THE CAT WHO
LIKED RAIN

Henning Mankell

First published in Great Britain by
Andersen Press Limited
This Large Print edition published by
BBC Audiobooks
by arrangement with
Andersen Press Limited 2010

ISBN: 978 1405 664042

British Library Cataloguing in Publication Data

Printed and bound in Great Britain by
CPI Antony Rowe, Chippenham and Eastbourne

THE CAT W   N

ONE

Lukas woke up suddenly.

When he opened his eyes, the room was almost completely dark. As he was still afraid of the dark, his mum used to leave a small light on every night. Lukas looked at the old alarm clock standing on the floor beside his bed. He wasn't absolutely sure about telling the time yet, but he thought it was five o'clock—and that was much too early. Nothing would happen until seven o'clock. He pulled the covers angrily over his head again, and tried to go back to sleep. But that was impossible. He was wide awake. And it wasn't easy to lie still. It was hard to have to wait for two more hours before anything happened when it was your birthday, and you were now seven years old.

He wondered what his present would be. Last year, on his sixth birthday, he'd guessed he would get a little tool box he'd seen in a shop window. That was what he'd asked for. The day

1

before his birthday his dad had come home with a parcel that rattled. That made Lukas certain he was going to get his tool box. But he didn't tell anybody he knew what it was. A surprise had to be a surprise, even if you happened to know what was in the parcel.

But this year, he didn't know. The problem was that he'd said he wanted so many things. He hadn't been able to make up his mind what he wanted most of all. That was probably why he'd woken up so early. He was nervous, in case he was given something he didn't want.

Lukas drummed his fingers on the blue and white wallpaper with a pattern made up of sailing boats. His head was full of thoughts jumping backwards and forwards.

He thought it was pretty special, being seven years old. Not least because his big brother, who was called Markus but known to everybody as Whirlwind, was now exactly twice as old as he was. Whirlwind was fourteen.

Lukas started giggling as he lay in bed. If Whirlwind was twice as old as

Lukas, shouldn't he also be twice as tall? But that would make him nearly six foot six. And his eyes ought to be twice as big as well. As big as saucers. Or maybe he ought to have twice as many eyes? Four instead of two? No, that was a silly idea, even if it was funny. Whirlwind wouldn't be at all pleased if he knew Lukas thought he had four eyes. Whirlwind got angry very easily, especially with Lukas. You always had to think carefully before you said or did anything.

The thoughts kept on jumping around inside Lukas's head. Now he was thinking about his dad, who was a lorry driver. Often when he came home there was a smell of a farmyard about him. Then Lukas knew he'd been taking some pigs or calves to the slaughterhouse. Other times, he might smell of something quite different.

Lukas always liked to try to guess what his dad had been carrying in his lorry when he came home in the evening. He would go out into the garage and sniff at the overalls hanging on a hook in there. Then he would go to the television room where his dad was lying on the sofa, waiting for his dinner to be ready. Lukas tried telling him what he thought his load had been and asked if he was right. Sometimes he'd guess right, but at other times he'd be completely wrong. He'd been wrong yesterday. When Lukas sniffed at his dad's overalls, he thought he could smell oil and petrol. He'd guessed that his dad had been delivering things to lots of petrol stations. But he'd been wrong. His dad smelled of oil because the lorry had broken down, and he'd been forced to lean over the engine with various tools in order to mend it.

Lukas's dad was called Axel. Axel Johanson, and that's why Lukas was also called Johanson.

'Axel Johanson and Lukas Johanson,' said Lukas out loud as he lay in bed, drumming his fingers on the wallpaper. But he was careful not to speak *too* loudly. That might wake his mum up, and he didn't want that as she would realise he was lying awake and couldn't get to sleep.

Now his thoughts jumped over to

her. Her name was Beatrice Aurore, and she was much younger than Axel. She wasn't at all like him, in fact. Axel was big and strong and had a very loud voice, but Beatrice was small and slim and spoke very quietly. It often sounded as if she was whispering. Axel spent all day from early in the morning driving his lorry around, and didn't come home until five in the evening. Beatrice stayed at home all day, except when she needed to go shopping.

She prepared meals and did the cleaning, and sometimes she would paint one of the old wooden chairs she used to buy at auctions during the summer. Lukas had never been able to understand why she was so fond of repainting old chairs. Axel probably couldn't either, but he never said anything.

Lukas thought he had two smashing parents. The best thing of all was that there were two of them. A lot of his friends only had one. If you had two parents, you could always ask twice for something you wanted. If one of them said no, you could ask the other one.

And then the answer might be yes. For instance, one of them might say no when you wanted to go out and play after dark. If Mum said no, he could always ask Dad instead. Lukas had realised that the best time to ask his mum for something dodgy was when she was busy painting an old chair. She was nearly always in a good humour then, and Lukas knew that she often didn't even hear what it was he was asking for. The worst time to ask her for something was when his dad wasn't around. She always said no then. With his dad, it was much harder to know when it was a good time to ask for something, and when it was better to keep quiet. And sometimes his dad would forbid him to do something he'd previously been given permission to do.

Parents can be difficult, Lukas thought. But even more difficult was having a brother older than yourself. Lukas sometimes felt angry when he thought about Whirlwind always being older than he was. No matter how much he grew, no matter how many years passed by, Whirlwind would always be older than Lukas. That was unfair, but there was nothing anybody could do about it.

Lukas sat up in bed. He looked at the clock again.

'Go faster,' he said to the hands. 'Run.'

But they didn't move any faster.

He would have to do something to make it seven o'clock. Maybe he ought to tiptoe into his parents' bedroom and move the hands on their alarm clock forward? No, they would notice. And besides, his dad didn't like getting up any earlier than necessary.

Lukas lay down again and continued thinking about Whirlwind. That was another thing that was unfair: his brother had a nickname, but nobody called Lukas anything other than Lukas. Whoever it was that had given Markus the name Whirlwind was a mystery. He'd simply been called that, always. And Whirlwind really was a whirlwind. He was incapable of standing still, and when he sat down at the table, he never stopped wriggling and squirming. But Lukas thought his brother must have been given that name because he was so brilliant on a skateboard. Nobody anywhere in Rowan Tree Road, where they lived, was as good as Whirlwind on a skateboard. He'd tried a few times to teach Lukas how to ride a skateboard—there were occasions when Whirlwind was the best big brother anybody could possibly ask for. But Lukas found it hard, and Whirlwind soon lost patience with him.

It seemed to Lukas that he would never be as good on a skateboard as Whirlwind. He'd have to find something else he was just as good at. But what might that be? He didn't know, and found it hard to think it through, because what he was most interested in just now was what his birthday present was going to be. He checked the time again. Another hour to go before his parents would wake up.

What had they bought for him? He'd mentioned new ice skates and a computer game, but he didn't really think he'd get either of those things.

He hoped they hadn't bought him some new clothes. That would be an awful present. You can't play with new clothes.

Another awful present would be something his parents considered to be useful. A bedside light, for instance, or a chair. Or worse still, a carpet.

Just think, if they gave him a carpet! He'd find it very hard to look pleased.

Every morning, when he woke up, he'd have to see this useful carpet lying on the floor next to his bed, but it would be absolutely useless for doing anything with. Carpets bought by your parents would never be able to fly. All they could do was lie on the floor—and if you were unlucky you could trip over them and bash your head.

Lukas suddenly got it into his head that he was going to be given a carpet. He was so sure that he became extremely angry. He wouldn't be able to swap it, either. Which of his friends would want a carpet? And needless to say, Whirlwind would nearly die laughing.

'It's not fair,' he said out loud. 'I

9

don't want a new carpet.' Then he thought about Whirlwind again. There was so much that was unfair. Whirlwind's birthday was in high summer, when you could sit out in the garden. Why should Lukas have to celebrate his birthday in March, when there was always slush everywhere and it was usually so cold? You couldn't sit out in the garden when it was raining or snowing!

You ought to be able to decide things yourself, Lukas thought. The date of your birthday, your name, what you were good at.

That was what he would ask for next year. A new birthday!

He checked the clock again. The hands had hardly moved.

Time passed so slowly.

Then he fell asleep, without noticing.

He didn't hear the alarm clock ring in his parents' bedroom. He didn't wake up until the light went on in his own room, and they were standing there, singing 'Happy Birthday To You!'

And then he received his present.

10

TWO

At first Lukas was disappointed.

When he woke up and heard his mum and dad singing at the side of his bed, all they had with them was a large cardboard box. It didn't even have any wrapping paper and ribbon round it. Lukas thought it looked like one of the boxes stored in the garage, full of old shoes. It didn't help that Mum was carrying a tray with a cake and seven burning candles. Lukas stared at the cardboard box. Why was he being given a cardboard box full of old shoes as a birthday present? He could feel his lower lip starting to tremble, and it felt warm behind his eyes. But he didn't want to start crying, he didn't want to show that he was disappointed. Dad might be angry. He didn't like people being sad when it wasn't necessary, as he used to say. Lukas also wondered why Whirlwind wasn't there. Was he still asleep, even though it was his little brother's birthday? The important day

11

when he became exactly twice as old as Lukas? But just as Lukas started thinking about Whirlwind, in he came. He was wearing only one slipper, and looked half asleep.

'Good, now we can all sing,' said Axel in his booming voice. He led them into a repeat version of 'Happy Birthday To You' so loud that the windowpanes rattled. You could hardly hear Beatrice, but Lukas could see that she was moving her lips. And she was smiling. Lukas thought that it couldn't just be old shoes in the cardboard box. His parents weren't as cruel as that. But he became worried again when he looked at Whirlwind. His brother wasn't singing at all. He just stood there, grinning at Lukas. Nobody could grin like Whirlwind. The way he grinned made you angry and sad and frightened, all at the same time. Obviously, Lukas thought, he knows what's in the box. He knows it's a pair of old shoes.

Lukas started to wonder if he ought to run away. If all he got for his birthday was a pair of old shoes, that must mean that Mum and Dad and Whirlwind didn't love him any more. And so he would run away. He'd go to somewhere where you were given proper parcels with wrapping paper and ribbon when it was your birthday.

Then Lukas heard something.

*   *   *

It was a different sort of sound forcing its way through his father's booming voice.

What was it? There it was again. It sounded as if something was squeaking. Then suddenly, just as 'Happy Birthday' was finished, the cardboard box started moving. It started jumping up and down, the lid was shaking, as if the box had turned into a saucepan full of boiling water.

Lukas stared at the box. That couldn't be a pair of old shoes. There was something moving inside there. And suddenly, that something popped up out of the box, something completely black. What was it? Lukas couldn't see at first. Then it dawned on

13

him that it was a paw. A black paw. And then a head appeared, and Lukas realised he'd been given a cat as a birthday present. A black cat that was now clambering out of the box. It jumped down from the lid, it was black all over, except for a white tip on its tail, and it looked at Lukas and squeaked.

Then it peed on his dad's foot.

Axel burst out laughing. 'You'll have to house-train it,' he said. 'It will need a box with some sand in, what's called a litter tray, where it can pee. Many Happy Returns, Lukas. You're a big boy now.'

'Many Happy Returns,' said Beatrice. (It was always like that in Lukas's home. First Dad said something, then Beatrice repeated it.)

'It mustn't come into my room,' said Whirlwind sternly. 'I don't want it breaking anything.'

'My cat won't break anything,' said Lukas angrily. 'And in any case, it doesn't want to go into your room.'

Whirlwind was just going to reply when Axel held his hand up.

'Come on, cut out this nonsense,' he said. 'It's Lukas's birthday. Let's have a slice of cake.'

And that's what they did. But Lukas hardly noticed what the cake tasted like: he was too busy watching the kitten, which had started exploring the room. It crawled under the bed then suddenly reappeared from behind the chest of drawers. It kept squeaking, and Beatrice said it was probably still looking for its mother.

'Now you've become a cat's mummy,' said Whirlwind with a satisfied smirk.

Lukas said nothing. But he thought that he'd teach the cat to hiss at Whirlwind whenever he said something stupid.

Mind you, he wasn't really bothered about Whirlwind just now. What had happened was so special that it hadn't really sunk in yet. Could it really be true? Yes, it was true. He had a kitten. He'd thought he would never have a pet of his own. When he'd asked for one, his dad had said that pets were far too much trouble, and you needed to be grown up in order to look after a cat or a dog. So Lukas had given up hope. When Dad spoke so firmly, things usually turned out like what he'd said. But now he'd been given a cat after all, a kitten that was black all over.

'What's its name?' Lukas asked.

'You'll have to give it a name yourself,' said Axel.

'I hope it's not a she,' said Whirlwind. 'We don't want it having loads of kittens.'

'It's a he,' said Axel. 'Shouldn't you be leaving for school soon?'

Whirlwind disappeared into his room without answering. Lukas was relieved to be rid of him. Whirlwind could be difficult sometimes.

'Well,' said Axel. 'What do you have to say?'

'Thank you,' said Lukas. 'Thank you very much.'

'You mustn't ever forget that you have a cat,' said Beatrice. 'He needs to have food every day, and you'll have to play with him. And change the sand in the litter tray. You're a big boy now, Lukas. Seven years old.'

'I'll look after him,' said Lukas.

16

'Anyway, I'd better be going,' said Axel. 'By the way, what did you think, when we came in with an old cardboard box?'

'I thought I was going to get a pair of old shoes,' said Lukas.

Axel gave him a wink.

'I saw your lower lip starting to tremble,' he said. 'But of course we weren't going to give you a pair of old shoes!'

'Of course not,' said Beatrice.

They went out of the room and left Lukas alone with his cat for the first time.

When he lifted him up, he gave a little squeak. Then he started playing with one of the buttons on his pyjama jacket.

At that moment, Lukas just knew that he was in love with this cat. He'd often wondered what it would be like, being in love with something. Now he knew. He'd got something for his birthday that he'd never even dared to dream about.

He was interrupted by Whirlwind barging in through the door.

17

'It's not allowed in my room,' he said. 'Don't forget that!'

'You must knock before you come into my room,' said Lukas. 'Look, you've frightened him!'

'A dog would have been better,' said Whirlwind. Then he left and slammed the door shut.

Lukas guessed that Whirlwind was only jealous. That wasn't a bad thing. Now Whirlwind could find out what it felt like. It was usually Lukas who felt jealous, because Whirlwind was allowed to do much more than he was. Now he could have some of his own medicine.

It seemed to Lukas that today marked the start of something different. Having a cat of your own that you were responsible for—that was something tremendous, something important. He must start by finding a name for the cat. What could you call a cat that was completely black? He wondered if he ought to have the same name as he did, Lukas. That could be good when Mum or Dad shouted: they would both come. But what would happen when Whirlwind shouted? That would be bound to cause problems, because he'd said the cat wasn't allowed in his room. No, Lukas would have to think of a different name. He looked at the cat, who had lain down on the middle of his pillow and fallen asleep. He was a completely black patch on the white pillow. And then it struck him what name the cat must have. Lukas didn't know of anything that was as black as the night.

Obviously, his cat would be called Night.

Now he had the only cat in the whole world called Night.

He lay down with his head next to the cat, and started stroking him. He immediately started purring.

'Night,' said Lukas. 'I have a cat called Night. I have you.'

Then Lukas fell asleep, and when his mum wondered why it was so quiet in his room and popped her head round the door, only Night was awake. Lukas was fast asleep.

From that day on, Lukas thought of hardly anything apart from his cat.

Night was a remarkable cat. Although he could only miaow, or squeak when he was hungry, it seemed to Lukas that he always understood what he'd said. Lukas had made up his mind that if he couldn't teach the cat to talk, he would have to learn the cat's language. Then they could go out into the world together.

He had never imagined he'd get such a wonderful present when he celebrated his seventh birthday.

THREE

And so Lukas began his new life with Night.

It was soon clear to him that everything had changed since Night joined the household. Every morning when Lukas woke up, it was Night who'd woken him. He would jump up onto the bed when he thought Lukas had slept for long enough, and lie down on his face. Deep down in his dreams, Lukas could hear a purring noise: he would slowly wake up and open his eyes. The fur was so soft, and there was a smell of leaves and rain about Night.

The only problem was that the cat couldn't tell the time. He sometimes woke Lukas up at four in the morning. Lukas tried to explain to Night that it was too early, and that he wanted to sleep longer than that. But Night just carried on playing, and when Lukas pulled the covers over his head, Night would continue to tug away at the sheets and bite Lukas's toes. Lukas had no choice but to get up, go to the kitchen and pour out some milk for Night, in the saucer on the floor next to the cooker. Then he would close the door and hurry back to bed. Night would sit in the kitchen, squealing and squeaking, but there was nobody to let him out until Beatrice and Axel got up to make breakfast.

Needless to say, Whirlwind had argued about where Night's litter tray ought to be. At first, Lukas had thought that the best place would be in the kitchen, where it would be easy to clear up any sand that Night had scratched and kicked onto the floor. But then Whirlwind started complaining about the smell being so awful that he couldn't eat. Lukas hadn't noticed any smell at all, and neither Axel nor Beatrice had mentioned any such thing until Whirlwind started going on about it. Eventually, Axel grew annoyed and said that Lukas should have the litter tray in his room. That was when Lukas resolved to teach Night to hiss every time Whirlwind spoke. But the main thing was that Night should grow up a bit. He was still only a kitten that jumped and scampered around, climbed up the curtains and played around with all the shoes in the hall.

For some time after Night had arrived on the scene, he wasn't allowed out. Axel said he needed to get used to his new home first. Otherwise there was a risk that he might run away. And Lukas was scared that somebody might steal his cat if he showed itself outside the house. Several times when Lukas shouted for Night and he didn't appear, Lukas was afraid that the

22

kitten might somehow have found its way out and vanished. Then his heart started pounding, exactly like when he'd woken up out of a nightmare. He shouted for Night, searched the whole house, but there was no sign of him.

Lukas soon discovered where Night used to hide away when he wanted to be left in peace and go to sleep. He would often lie on the laundry basket in the bathroom. Sometimes he would be hiding in Axel's wardrobe. Occasionally he would jump up and lie on top of one of the highest cupboards in the kitchen. But sometimes, Lukas couldn't find him anywhere. When Beatrice noticed that Lukas was so upset that his lower lip started trembling, she would help him to look. And they would eventually find him. On one occasion Night had managed to get into the garage, and bedded down in a box full of rubbish. But every time Lukas found Night, he was so pleased that all he could do was to sit absolutely still, gazing at his very own cat. That was something quite new for Lukas—being so happy that the only thing it was possible to do was to sit quite still. Before that, being happy meant shouting out loud, or jumping for joy. But now that Night had entered Lukas's life, something totally new had happened.

The big problem was Whirlwind. Lukas was soon absolutely sure that Whirlwind really was jealous because his little brother had a cat. Whirlwind sometimes pulled Night's tail. Not hard enough to really hurt, but enough to make Night squeal. That made Lukas so furious that he started punching at Whirlwind, who naturally did nothing but laugh. If Axel was at home, he sometimes became so angry that it all ended by Lukas taking Night into his room and shutting the door. He had noticed that Whirlwind was careful to annoy him and Night when their father was at home, and preferably when Dad was tired or in a bad mood. Lukas suspected that Whirlwind hoped Dad would become so fed up with all the messing about that he would refuse to allow Night inside the house.

That was a horrible thought. Lukas

didn't know what he could do about that, apart from always keeping a little parcel of food in the fridge. If Night wasn't allowed in the house, Lukas wouldn't want to be there either. They would go off together.

Once, when his dad had been in a really bad mood and complained about all the arguments taking place every day, Lukas had asked his mum if Dad now regretted having given Lukas Night as a present. Mum calmed him down and said that of course, they would never even dream of taking the cat away from him. Lukas thought that was probably right. But then again, he wasn't quite sure. Every day he made up his little parcel of food, and hid it behind the milk at the very back of the fridge.

*   *   *

The best thing would have been if Whirlwind had been given a cat of his own. Or perhaps even better, a different animal. A dog probably wouldn't be a good idea. But some

25

goldfish, perhaps, or canaries? Lukas wondered how he could be cunning enough to fix things so that he could give Whirlwind an animal as a birthday present. One day when he was out shopping with Beatrice, he persuaded her to take him into a pet shop. But he was depressed when he saw how expensive an aquarium was, even though it was the smallest one in the shop. And he'd never be able to afford a bird cage, complete with birds.

But Night was giving Lukas more than enough to think about. Every new day brought with it a new problem. Even so, every day made Lukas think that his cat was the best thing that had ever happened to him.

Every night, before he went to sleep, Lukas would lie in bed and talk to Night, who was generally curled up on the pillow beside him. Every time Lukas closed his eyes, it was like closing an invisible door and entering a new world that belonged only to him and Night. It was a secret world that nobody else knew about. Even if it only existed inside his own head, it was

26

absolutely real. You could wander around inside that world behind his closed eyelids, and everything looked just the same as it always did—despite the fact that everything was different.

It seemed to Lukas that this secret world was a fairytale world, full of trolls. There were troll streets and troll houses, troll shops and troll skateboards. In this secret world everybody spoke a troll language, and wore troll clothes. Sometimes a troll sun shone, and sometimes troll rain fell. Everybody ate troll food and played troll games. Laughed troll laughter and got troll scratches when they tripped up and scrubbed their knees. Everything was exactly the same as in the real world. But when Lukas put the word 'troll' in front of things, everything became secret and exciting. He was lying in bed, dreaming about all the adventures he, Troll-Lukas, and Troll-Night, would be able to experience together. As soon as summer came, and it was warm again.

And summer did come eventually. Lukas and Whirlwind helped Dad to spring-clean the caravan parked next to the garage. They scrubbed and rinsed with the hose pipe until they were soaking wet through. Then one day in early June, they towed the caravan to the camping site by the lake where they always used to spend every summer. Before Axel had his holidays, they would spend Friday, Saturday and Sunday out there. But once the holidays started, they lived in the caravan for a whole month.

Lukas had been dreading the first journey Night would have to make in the car. Would he be nervous? Would he try to run away? But to his great relief, Axel had thought about the problem and one day came home with a collar and lead for Night.

'Now you'll have to teach the cat how to wear a collar, and go for walks on a lead,' he said.

Lukas found a black laundry pen and wrote Night's name on the collar. For safety's sake he also drew a skull, so that nobody would dare to try to steal Night.

Night didn't like wearing a collar at

all. Nor was it easy to teach Night how to go for walks on a lead. All Night did was to chew the lead and get tangled up in it. Whirlwind watched what was happening, with a broad grin on his face. But Lukas didn't give up. He knew that Night would have to learn, or there would be problems.

*   *   *

It was a long, hot summer in the caravan. Lukas took Night to the little cabin he'd built the previous year—it was really only a gap between two big rocks, with a roof and a back and a door. It had collapsed during the winter, and split open in two places. Lukas made a new roof using branches and pine twigs with lots of needles, and when you stood outside and looked at it, it wasn't easy to see that there was a cabin there at all. Lukas crept inside, and let Night off the lead. They often stayed in there for hours on end. Lukas would close his eyes and imagine that they were far, far away in the troll world. Only when he heard Beatrice shouting to say that they should come and eat would he put Night back on his lead, and crawl out of the cabin.

'You'll have to shout for Night as well,' he said to Mum. 'He's also hungry.'

'Oh, I forgot that,' said Beatrice. 'I'll try to remember next time.'

Whirlwind had his own set of friends, and didn't have time to annoy Lukas and Night during the summer. He spent most nights in a tent with his pals, and so Lukas could be alone in his little bed in the caravan with Night. Axel and Beatrice didn't mind Night jumping up onto their bed during the night. Lukas grew more and more calm, the longer summer went on. Nobody was going to take his cat away from him!

Lukas also had friends of his own who lived in other caravans in long rows next to the lake shore. When he was playing with his friends, he would leave Night in the caravan, and Beatrice promised to look after him and not let him out.

The only thing wrong with summer

was that it didn't last long enough. Lukas tried not to think about the fact that it was August already. He would be starting school soon, and he was both looking forward to it and also worrying about what it would be like. It was best not to think about it at all. But days passed by, and Axel sometimes commented on how it was already getting darker in the evenings.

Lukas sometimes wondered why there weren't any schools for cats. Why shouldn't cats also need to learn various things? He tried to imagine a row of little cats at desks, putting their paws up and saying their names to a cat teacher at the front.

One night, before going to sleep, he made up his mind that he would start a school of his own with Night. He would try to teach him the same things that he'd been learning at school.

Then he fell asleep; and a few days later they moved back to Rowan Tree Road. They left the caravan by the lake, because they would still be going back there every weekend.

But Axel's holidays were over, there

was nothing anybody could do about that. And in three weeks' time, Lukas would be starting school.

Lukas thought they would be three very long weeks. Three more weeks to go before his very first day at school came around.

But nothing turned out as he had expected.

One morning, Night disappeared.

FOUR

Night disappeared on a perfectly normal day.

When Lukas woke up in the morning he knew that it was Thursday and that he would be having pancakes for dinner. He stretched out in his bed, and felt around on the covers to see if Night was lying there, asleep. Then he remembered that Night had woken him up long before dawn. Feeling tired, and perhaps also a bit angry at having been disturbed, Lukas had shuffled into the kitchen with the cat dancing around his

32

feet, and placed a little herring in his food bowl. Night hardly ever drank milk now, he'd been eating proper food for some time. Lukas then closed the kitchen door, went back to bed and fell asleep immediately.

But when Lukas got up and went to the kitchen, Night wasn't there. Lukas shouted for him, but there was no response. He put a chair in front of the work surface and clambered up so that he could see the tops of the kitchen cupboards. Night wasn't lying there either. Lukas put the chair back, and thought that his dad must have forgotten to close the kitchen door when he'd finished breakfast. Night had no doubt hidden himself away somewhere else. Lukas still wasn't worried. He'd begun to get used to the fact that Night was like himself: sometimes he just wanted to be left in peace.

As Night didn't have a room of his own to which he could retire and close the door, he had to keep looking for new hiding places. Lukas had often thought that Night was much better than he was at discovering new hideaways that were difficult to find.

Lukas sat down at the kitchen table, drank some milk and ate a sandwich. He could hear his mother working in the laundry room. There was a whining noise a bit like an aeroplane's engine when the washing machine was in operation. Lukas thought that Night had no doubt gone with Beatrice into the laundry room. He liked playing with the heap of dirty linen.

When he'd finished his breakfast Lukas went to the laundry room.

'Is Night here?' he asked.

'I don't know,' said Beatrice. 'I think I saw him not long ago. Yes, he must be around here somewhere.'

Lukas went to his room and got dressed. When he looked out of the window, it was obvious that today was going to be spent indoors. It was windy and raining, and drops were pattering away at the windowpanes. He pressed his nose against the glass and wondered what sort of load his dad would have in the lorry today. He hoped the windscreen wipers were working properly. Lukas was sometimes worried in case his dad had an accident with that big lorry of his.

He could hear that it was still quiet in Whirlwind's room. Sometimes Whirlwind would sleep in until ten o'clock. Lukas often wished that Whirlwind would sleep all day, every day. Then he wouldn't need to worry about Whirlwind being angry with him, or with Night.

Then he started looking properly for Night. First he checked all the usual hiding places he knew about. No sign of Night. Then he checked every room, one after the other. He crept around as quietly as possible, because he usually turned the search into a game. He didn't want to frighten Night, he wanted to try to move so quietly that Night wouldn't hear him and prick his ears or wake up.

But Night wasn't there. There was no sign of him.

And suddenly, as if from nowhere, Lukas had that horrible feeling in his stomach. Night had disappeared. Lukas felt frightened, just as if he'd been lying

35

asleep and been woken up by a nightmare.

'I can't find Night,' he said to Beatrice, who was busy scraping the paint off an old chair.

'He'll turn up as soon as he feels hungry,' she said.

It was at that very moment Lukas knew for certain that Night had disappeared. The feeling was so strong that he couldn't brush it aside.

'He's run away,' he said.

Beatrice smiled at him.

'You always think that when he's hidden himself away somewhere and you can't find him at first,' she said.

'No, he's gone,' said Lukas again, and his voice was shaking.

Beatrice looked at him in surprise. She'd heard the unsteadiness in his voice, just like it sounded when he was about to start crying.

'Of course he hasn't run away,' she said. 'This morning when your dad and I were having breakfast he was scampering around in the kitchen. There were fish bones all over the floor. You don't need to worry. He wouldn't go out when it's raining like this, now, would he? Cats don't like rain, surely you know that?'

Just for a moment Lukas felt a little calmer. It was true what Mum said, Night didn't like water. Once, and only once, Lukas had tried to give Night a bath—and had decided he would never do it again. Night had wriggled and scratched and in the end Lukas had been covered in water and soap. Night had hidden underneath the sofa in the living room, as far in as possible, and it was several hours before he came out again.

So Lukas felt a bit calmer. But not for long. He searched through the house once again. This time he made as much noise as he possibly could, in an attempt to make Night appear. He also fetched a tin of cat food from the pantry and hit against it with a fork. Night usually recognised the noise, and would come bounding up, even if he'd only just finished eating.

But Night didn't appear. He was nowhere to be found. Eventually Beatrice joined in the search as well.

When Whirlwind finally woke up and saw how unhappy Lukas was, he also started calling for Night.

They spent all day searching, but there was no trace of Night. Lukas and Beatrice put on Wellington boots and rainwear, and went out. It was typical autumn weather, windy, and pools of water everywhere. They searched through every inch of the garden, and Beatrice also asked the neighbours if they'd seen Night. But they all shook their heads, nobody had seen him.

When Axel came home for dinner, he started looking as well. That was Lukas's last hope. If his dad couldn't find Night, nobody could.

But there was no sign of Night.

'How on earth was he able to get out of the house?' Axel wondered. 'And why has he chosen to run away on a day when it's been pouring with rain all the time?'

But Lukas didn't want to know why Night had disappeared. All he wanted was for somebody to help him find his cat. Axel and Beatrice and even Whirlwind tried to console him.

'He'll come back,' they said, over and over again.

'Night doesn't like getting wet,' said Lukas.

'A cat will cope with anything,' said Axel. 'They say a cat has nine lives. You don't need to worry. He'll come back.'

'I don't care if Night has nine lives or not,' said Lukas. 'I just want him to be here.'

'You're bound to get a new cat if he has run away,' said Whirlwind. That was the stupidest thing he could possibly have said. He didn't mean any harm, of course. But as far as Lukas was concerned, it made it sound as if Night no longer existed, that he was no longer alive, that he might even never have lived. Had it all been no more than a dream? Had he dreamt about that birthday present he'd been given over six months ago? Had he been asleep all that time and only thought he was awake? Perhaps he had in fact received a carpet, or a box of old shoes?

'I don't want any other cat apart from

Night,' said Lukas, and now he couldn't stop himself from crying. 'There is only one cat in the whole world that I care about.'

That night Lukas didn't want to go to bed. He went from window to window, staring out into the darkness where the rain was pattering against the swaying street lights. He tried to force himself to see through the thick darkness, forcing Night to come back.

But the street was deserted. Night wasn't there.

When Lukas finally fell asleep on a chair in front of the living room window, Axel carried him into his mum's and dad's bedroom.

'It's best for him to sleep here with us until he wakes up,' he whispered.

'What can we do?' Beatrice wondered.

'I don't know,' said Axel. 'Let's just hope the cat comes back.'

*   *   *

But Night didn't come back the next day either. Beatrice wrote out a

number of little notices that she and
Lukas could attach to lampposts,
telegraph poles and notice boards, and
inside shops.

Runaway Cat
*Has anybody seen a black male cat with
a little white patch at the tip of its tail?
Please contact Rowan Tree Road 19.
Telephone 491408.
Reward.*

'Put a million kronor,' said Lukas.

'I can't do that,' said Beatrice. 'We
haven't got as much money as that.'

'Put it in any case,' said Lukas. 'Then
people will understand how much I
miss him.'

'They'll understand that even so,'
said Beatrice.

It continued raining the next day as
well, the second day with no sign of
Night. Lukas went with Beatrice to put
up the notices. When they got back
home again, Lukas asked for some
money so that he could go and buy a
comic. Beatrice thought it would be
good for him not to simply hang

around, wondering where Night had disappeared to. But Lukas didn't go to buy a comic. Instead he went back to all the places where they'd stuck up notices, and added an extra line at the end.

One milyen.

He wasn't sure how to spell it. He asked one of the checkout ladies at the mini-market how to spell the word 'million', but she had just snapped angrily at him and told him not to get in the way of paying customers. So he went into the street and asked old Trumlund, who used to sit there every day in a little hut selling raffle tickets for the local bowling club, how to spell 'million'.

'You spell it exactly as it sounds,' said Trumlund.

Lukas gave up the attempt to find out how to spell 'million'. He wrote it as he thought it sounded, and thought that whoever read it would understand anyway.

Then he went back home, shouting

for Night all the way.

'Didn't you buy your comic?' asked Beatrice in surprise.

'They'd sold out,' said Lukas.

'Didn't you buy anything else instead?' she wondered.

'I'm saving up until I've got a million,' he said.

That night Lukas made up his mind about two things. He would never give up until he'd found Night. He knew that Night needed him. He also made up his mind that if Night hadn't come back by the following morning, he would leave home and go looking for him. Maybe it would be easier to find Night if he tried to live like a cat does? Out in the night, all alone, slinking around in the shadows? Once he'd made up his mind, he went back to the living room and placed the chair in front of the window. Then he sat there all evening, staring out into the night.

Sometimes he would jump up from the chair. He thought he'd seen a pair of cat's eyes, glittering in the darkness. But then they faded away, and everything was black, everywhere was black.

'I shall find you, Night,' he said quietly to himself, so that nobody else could hear him. 'I know that something's happened. But I'll find you. I promise.'

*　　　*　　　*

That night Axel carried Lukas to his own bed, once he'd fallen asleep on the chair in front of the window.

The following day when Lukas woke up, it had more or less stopped raining. Ragged, grey clouds were chasing each other across the sky. Occasionally, between light showers of rain, the cold sun shone down on the streets, which were still very wet.

Lukas stood by the window in his room for ages, gazing out into the garden.

But Night hadn't come back.

Night was still missing.

FIVE

The third day after Night's disappearance turned out quite differently from what Lukas had expected.

What on earth had he sparked off?

Early in the morning the telephone started ringing, and people came knocking on the door carrying cats of every colour imaginable. An old lady came trudging through the rain with a cat that was orange from top to toe, and asked Axel—who was only half awake—if this was the cat that had run away.

'Eh?' said Axel. 'An orange cat? Our missing cat is black, apart from some white at the very tip of his tail.'

'Well,' said the old lady, 'maybe this is him even so?'

'No,' said Axel. 'But thank you for coming.'

As he closed the door, the telephone rang; Beatrice answered, and she had barely put the receiver down when it rang again. Axel didn't even have time to get dressed, as he was running backwards and forwards to the door all the time.

Black cats, grey cats, ugly cats, handsome cats, young cats, cats with evil eyes, cats that purred and rubbed up against your legs. They were all being carried in cardboard boxes, or inside raincoats.

'What's going on?' Axel wondered in the end. 'The whole town is coming with their cats to our house. What on earth did you write on those notices you stuck up yesterday?'

'That the missing cat was black with a little white patch at the tip of its tail,' said Beatrice. 'I don't understand why all these people are coming with cats that aren't even black.'

All this time, Lukas was fast asleep in bed, and had no idea about all these people who thought the cat they had found was Night. It wasn't until he'd got up and Axel had gone to work, leaving all the chaos behind, that he realised what he had started.

'Can you imagine how many people

there must be who can't read?' asked Beatrice with a sigh.

'I certainly think they can read,' said Lukas. 'I wrote on all the notices that the reward for finding Night was a million. I probably spelled it wrongly, but people must have understood even so.'

Beatrice was so surprised that she almost fell over one of the kitchen chairs.

'You did what, did you say?' she asked.

Lukas repeated what he had said.

'I told you I was going to buy a comic,' he said. 'But what I really did was to go round the notices and write in that the reward was a million kronor.'

Lukas was surprised to discover how easy it was to tell the truth. It was as if everything that had been so difficult before had been swept away, now that Night had disappeared. Since that was the only thing that mattered to Lukas, everything else became much easier.

Beatrice shook her head.

'Lukas,' she said slowly, 'why did you

do that?'

'I don't know,' Lukas said. 'I just had to.'

That was as far as they got, because there was another knock on the door.

'I haven't the strength to look at any more brown cats,' said Beatrice.

'I'll go,' said Lukas, leaving the kitchen.

When he opened the door he found a man standing there with a big bag hanging over one of his shoulders. Lukas wondered if the man had a cat hidden inside it.

'Is this where you can get a reward of a million kronor if you find a missing cat?' the man asked.

'Yes,' said Lukas.

The man laughed as he responded.

'Can a cat really be worth as much as that?' he asked.

'Yes,' said Lukas. 'Night is worth that much.'

'Night?'

'My cat is called Night.'

Beatrice arrived at that point.

'It's a misunderstanding, of course,' she said. 'We don't have a million to

48

pay as a reward.'

'I'm a journalist,' said the man. 'I thought I'd write something in the newspaper about this cat that's worth a million kronor.'

Beatrice was horrified.

'You can't do that,' she said. 'We've had people coming here all morning, bringing cats of every description you can think of. There'll be even more if you write about it in the newspaper. They might even come with other animals as well. Dogs and chickens and goodness only knows what else . . .'

'It would be great if there was something in the paper about it,' interrupted Lukas. 'Especially if there was a photograph of Night as well. Then lots of people will see him. Maybe one of the readers will recognise him? By the way, I have a million in toy money. I can use that to pay the reward.'

'Lukas,' said Beatrice, 'stop talking about money.'

But the journalist thought it would be a brilliant idea to write about Lukas and his cat, even if all that about such a big reward wasn't really true.

'I understand that you are so fond of your cat,' he said. 'I shall write about that. People like reading in the newspaper about people who are so fond of their missing pets.'

And so a photograph of Night appeared in the newspaper. Axel had taken it in the summer, when Night had been lying on Lukas's knee outside the caravan. The journalist wrote about Lukas, where he lived, and that he hoped somebody would soon find his Night.

But there was still no sign of Night.

Even so, Lukas could think about nothing else. He thought about how Night would be hungry and wet and cold, he thought about nasty people throwing stones at him or pulling his tail. He thought so hard about Night that he almost turned into a cat himself. It was as if he had acquired black fur and pointed ears. But most of all, he thought that the best way of protecting Night was for him to think about the cat all the time. As long as Night was there inside Lukas's head, he wouldn't be in danger.

When he'd gone to bed that night, and Beatrice had tucked him in, Lukas made up his mind once again that he would have to run away. He couldn't wait any longer, it would have to happen now.

But at the same time, he also thought of something else.

The currant bush.

The big, wild blackcurrant bush growing just outside the fence of Lukas's garden.

The currant bush where Night had so much liked to curl up when it was warm, and when he wanted to be left in peace and sleep. There was something special about that currant bush. It was growing all on its own, with no other bushes anywhere near. Axel had often said it ought to be cut down. But when Lukas asked why, his dad hadn't been able to give him an answer. It was as if currant bushes had to grow inside fences. They weren't allowed to be wild. It seemed to Lukas that it was a bit like dogs having to wear collars. A fence was a sort of collar that currant bushes had to have.

Night had liked that wild currant bush so very much. Lukas sometimes thought that what grew there in the early autumn was really troll black-currants. They were very special berries, with a secret.

If you ate them, you could see straight into the troll world without needing to shut your eyes first.

Lukas stayed in bed, thinking about that bush. Needless to say, that was where he ought to start looking for Night.

Why hadn't he realised that sooner!

Of course he would put Night's special food saucer there, the one with the blue hoop round it, with a crack at one point on the edge. That saucer would be bound to entice Night back again.

He felt that he needed to act right away. But when he slid out of bed and tiptoed to the door, he could hear that his parents were still up. They were watching some television programme or other. He could hear his father yawning. Lukas went back to bed. He would have to wait until they'd gone to bed and fallen asleep. Then he would be able to sneak out of the house with the saucer.

Eventually, everything fell silent. Lukas put some clothes on over the top of his pyjamas. Then he tiptoed into the kitchen and carefully opened the fridge. He almost burst into tears when he saw the open tin of cat food standing there on its own, behind a pack of butter. It seemed to him that what he was looking at was poor, abandoned Night, not a can of cat food with no lid.

He put everything that was left onto the saucer.

Then he wondered what to do with the empty tin. Mum would doubtless think it was odd. She had a remarkable ability to see everything that nobody ought to be able to see. That somebody had eaten the cat food even when Night wasn't there, for instance.

Lukas put some of the food from the saucer back into the can, and added a few drops of milk to make it look a bit more than it was. Then he closed the fridge door and tiptoed out into the hall. He listened to his father's snores as they came rolling out from the bedroom. Then he carefully unlocked the front door and put it on the latch so that he wouldn't be locked out when he'd closed it behind him.

It was still raining. It felt very cold, and Lukas shuddered. He wasn't wearing any socks. He'd just stuck his feet into his Wellingtons. It felt creepy in the dark garden. Lukas hesitated before daring to enter the darkness beyond the light cast by the lamp over the door.

The currant bush was a long way away in the darkness. When it was light, Lukas used to think it wasn't far at all to the fence. But now that it was dark, it felt as if the fence was as far away as a star in the sky. A black star that didn't glisten.

He didn't have a torch with him. But nevertheless, he would have to be brave and dare to walk into that darkness even so—and the splashing of the rain would prevent him from hearing if anybody came creeping up behind him.

But he had to do it. He needed to do it for Night's sake. He had to be brave, even if there was nothing so difficult as daring to do something you didn't dare do.

He closed his eyes tightly and ran through the darkness, holding tightly onto the saucer of food. He stumbled when he came to the fence, and spilled half the food. But he didn't dare to pick it up, he didn't even dare to look round. He clambered over the fence. He came to the currant bush, placed the saucer on the soaking wet ground, and ran back towards the welcoming light over the front door.

Then he went back to bed, his heart pounding.

He wasn't yet sure what was worse: Night having disappeared in the darkness, or him daring to do something he didn't dare to do.

He eventually fell asleep.

*　　　*　　　*

The next day, after he'd woken up, he

ran through the garden to the wild, mysterious currant bush—then stopped dead.

Night wasn't there.

But the saucer was empty.

SIX

Lukas stood absolutely still.

It was as if his heart had stopped beating. He couldn't stop looking at the empty saucer. So Night had come back. He'd returned to his currant bush, he'd found the saucer of food, and he'd eaten up everything that was there, because he was so hungry. Lukas couldn't possibly stand still any longer. Night must be somewhere close by.

'Night,' he shouted—no, he yelled. He yelled so loudly that a neighbour who was sweeping up fallen leaves jumped and almost dropped his rake.

Then Lukas started searching. He would have to find Night now. On the opposite side of the road, where they hadn't started building houses yet, there was a lot of high grass, bushes, and some trees. That's where Night must be. Lukas looked left and right, then ran over the road. And started looking for Night. Now that he was sure that Night wasn't far away, he wasn't frightened any more. He was so sure of himself that he could turn the search into a game. He imagined Night as a wild and dangerous predator who could only be tamed by Lukas. A red lion, he thought. The rare and highly dangerous red lion can only be found in the jungle on the other side of the River Rowan. Lukas picked up a broken-off branch lying in the ditch. He had a weapon now, and would be able to overcome the red lion.

At that very moment the postman arrived on his bicycle. Lucas ducked down behind a bush. The postman, dressed in blue, was one of the most dangerous of all enemies, and had to be avoided at all cost.

But the postman noticed Lukas and waved to him as he pedalled past.

One of the more friendly postmen, Lukas thought. There aren't many of them. But sometimes you get lucky.

Then he carried on searching. It was still a game, looking for the red lion. But the lion became more and more difficult to imagine, the more he searched for it. He started to feel frightened again, when he couldn't find Night. Eventually, the red lion had disappeared altogether, the tree branch was just a branch, and not a weapon; and there was still no sign of Night.

Suddenly, Lukas was angry with his cat. Why was he acting like this? Why didn't he come home?

Lukas went back over the street, taking with him the empty saucer, and went back to the house. He kicked off his boots and went into the kitchen, where his mum was. He felt a need to talk to her.

'Night's come back,' he said.

'Really?' said Beatrice in astonishment. 'Where is he?'

'I can't find him,' said Lucas. 'But he's come back home. I know he has. He ate the food I put out for him last night.'

Beatrice looked at him in surprise.

'Now I don't understand what you're talking about,' she said. 'What food?'

Lukas explained what he'd done the previous evening.

'You mean you went out in the middle of the night?' she said. 'And the saucer was empty this morning?'

Lukas nodded. Sometimes it took such a long time for parents to understand what their children were saying. Lukas wondered why parents always thought so much more slowly than children. Why was it so difficult for parents to understand things that were so simple and straightforward?

'There's no cat food left,' Lukas said. 'We'll have to buy another tin so that I can put out some more meat. And I'll be sitting out there, waiting until Night comes back.'

'Of course you will,' said Beatrice. 'Why don't you go to the shop and buy whatever you need. It's marvellous news that Night has come back again.'

'No, you can go to the shops,' said Lukas. 'I'm going to sit waiting by the currant bush.'

'Oh, come on! It's not all that

urgent,' said Beatrice.

'I'm not going to give Night another chance of escaping,' said Lukas. 'You can do the shopping.'

Beatrice went to the shop. Meanwhile, Lukas carried out one of the kitchen chairs and sat down next to the currant bush. The neighbour who was raking up leaves gave Lukas a curious look. He couldn't resist asking why Lukas was sitting on a kitchen chair and staring at a currant bush.

'I'm just sitting and thinking,' said Lukas. He didn't want to say that he was sitting there, waiting for Night to come back. He was afraid that Night wouldn't show up if he seemed to be too certain that his cat really was hovering around in the background.

It's children who ought to be curious, he thought. Adults shouldn't stand by fences, asking unnecessary questions.

The neighbour shook his head in response to Lukas's answer, and continued raking up his leaves. And Lukas carried on waiting.

Beatrice came back and put some more cat food onto the saucer. Then she also wanted to wait and see if Night came back. But Lukas told her to go back indoors. He wanted to be alone.

It was cold, sitting there on the chair. Cold and boring. Lukas kicked away, and dug out a hole in the ground with his heels. But still Night didn't make an appearance.

Then it started raining again.

Beatrice came out and told him he'd catch a cold if he carried on sitting out there in the rain. But Lukas told her to bring him an umbrella. And his dad's sou'wester. Beatrice shook her head and sighed. But she did as he'd asked.

Lukas sat out there in the rain, holding an umbrella over his head. The neighbour had stopped sweeping up leaves when it started raining, but Lukas could see him standing in the window of his house, keeping watch.

In the end, Lukas couldn't sit waiting on the chair any longer. Maybe it was better if he didn't sit there? Maybe Night was a bit afraid that Lukas would be angry with him for running away? Maybe it was better to do what the neighbour had done, and stand looking out of a window?

Lukas decided that this would be best, and carried the chair back to the kitchen. Beatrice made him a sandwich. But Lukas didn't have time to sit eating in the kitchen. He sat on a chair by the window and stared at the currant bush. He suddenly noticed something moving behind the currant bush. He pressed his nose up against the windowpane. Had he been mistaken? No—there it was again. Something moving. Something black . . .

Lukas yelled out loud and raced into the hall. He didn't have time to put on his Wellingtons, but rushed out in his stockinged feet, ran over the soaking wet lawn, climbed over the fence and staggered up to the currant bush as fast as he possibly could.

Then he discovered that it wasn't Night.

It was another black cat. But it didn't have a white tip on its tail. It was another cat eating Night's food—and perhaps this was the cat that had eaten the food Lukas had put out the previous night as well?

Lukas was so angry that he aimed a kick at the cat. It ran away, of course. Lucas picked up a stone and threw it at the cat. It gave a squeak when the stone hit it. Then Lukas picked up a handful of gravel and threw it—but the cat ran over the road and vanished into the bushes where the red lion normally lurked.

Beatrice had followed him out and came up, carrying his Wellingtons.

'What on earth are you doing?' she said, and sounded angry. 'Are you throwing stones at the cat?'

'It ate Night's food,' said Lukas angrily.

'It couldn't know that it was meant for Night,' said Beatrice.

'But it's Night's saucer,' said Lukas.

'That's enough of this nonsense,' said Beatrice. 'Put your Wellingtons on this instant. Then we're going in.'

Night didn't come back home that day either. Lukas didn't bother sitting by the window any more, staring at the currant bush. He shut himself away in his room.

What could he do?

Night had been missing for over three whole days now. Lukas tried to understand why Night had wandered out into the rain. What had happened? Had Night been upset about something? Had he run away?

It seemed to Lukas that it wasn't easy to understand what went on inside a cat's head. Lukas knew how he behaved when he was angry or upset or happy. But he wasn't at all sure how Night reacted in such circumstances. Lukas knew that Night's tail would be upright when he was pleased and contented, and that he would rub up against Lukas's legs, and that he would purr. But what would Night do when he was upset?

Lukas didn't know the answer to the questions he asked. And when he asked Beatrice, she didn't know either.

'You ask such difficult questions,' she said. 'I don't think anybody can answer them.'

'Not even Dad?' Lukas asked.

'Not even Dad,' said Beatrice.

'How come that there can be

64

questions without any answers?' Lukas wondered.

'You tell me,' said Beatrice. 'That's something I also ask myself at times.'

Lukas went back to his room, and continued thinking. There was another possibility that he preferred not to think about. Somebody might have stolen Night, bundled him into a box and run off with him. But who could be so nasty as to steal a cat? Who could possibly do anything like that?

Lukas had no idea what to do. He didn't think he'd have the strength to start school if Night didn't come back. He wondered how on earth he'd be able to live a whole life, become an adult, and later on an old man, without knowing what had happened to Night.

That night, when he'd gone to bed, he decided to ask Whirlwind to help him. Perhaps the pair of them might be able to work together and find out where Night was? Lukas wasn't at all sure that Whirlwind would want to cooperate. But he'd been unusually quiet since Night had disappeared.

Perhaps he would help to search,

despite everything?

The thought of talking to Whirlwind made Lukas feel a bit calmer. He curled up under the covers, and tried to imagine Night lying next to his face.

SEVEN

The next day, it had finally stopped raining.

Whirlwind was just about to go out with his skateboard when Lukas entered the hall.

'My cat didn't come back last night either,' said Lukas.

'So I noticed,' said Whirlwind. 'But I've heard of cats being lost for several years and then suddenly turning up again.'

'I don't want to wait for ten years,' said Lukas.

Then Whirlwind said something that astonished Lukas.

'I thought we could help you to look for the cat,' he said.

So Whirlwind had actually been

thinking the same thing as Lukas! That he should help to look for Night!

It dawned on Lukas that he hadn't realised until now that he had the best big brother it's possible to have. He wasn't so difficult and troublesome as Lukas had thought after all.

'Of course we shall look for the cat,' said Whirlwind again. 'We'll start looking this very day.'

'Who's we?' wondered Lukas.

'My mates,' said Whirlwind. 'We're going to search every single garden, every single place where he might have hidden himself away.'

Whirlwind had four or five friends who all had skateboards. They used to go skateboarding together, practised together, and competed against each other. Whirlwind was the leader because he was the best skateboarder. Lukas could imagine them rushing along on their skateboards, pausing to look for Night, then racing along to the next garden. The thought of Whirlwind and his friends helping Lukas to find his cat filled his heart with warmth. He felt an urge to hug Whirlwind, but he didn't. Whirlwind didn't like it when their mother sometimes gave him a hug. He was sure to be angry if Lukas tried to do the same.

'I'd like to join you in looking,' said Lukas.

'You don't have a skateboard,' said Whirlwind. 'But you can be our mechanic.'

Lukas didn't really know what a mechanic did. And he didn't want to ask because Whirlwind didn't like being asked silly questions. He'd have to try to find out by other means.

'Of course I'll be your mechanic,' he said. 'Shall I start right away?'

'Fetch a bucket and a rag and some washing powder,' said Whirlwind. 'You can clean our skateboards when they get dirty. We'll be meeting at nine o'clock in the street next to the playground.'

He was in a hurry now. As soon as his mum had left the kitchen, he opened the door of the cleaning cupboard and took out a bucket, a scouring cloth and a packet of washing powder. Then he opened the window and dropped them down onto the ground. He half-filled the bucket from the tap outside the house—it would be too heavy if he put in any more water. Even so, he had trouble in carrying it as far as the playground. He wondered how much washing powder he ought to add. He eventually decided it was better to use too much rather than too little, so he used the whole packet. He stirred it with a piece of wood, and soon the foam had piled up like a steeple on top of the bucket. He was afraid he'd used too much. But the first of Whirlwind's friends was approaching already. Lukas began cleaning his skateboard with the cloth after dipping it in the frothy water.

'Have you found Night yet?' he asked.

'That kind of thing takes time,' said Whirlwind's friend. 'Hurry up, now!'

When Lukas had finished, Whirlwind's friend set off again. And then the next skateboard arrived, ready to be cleaned.

And so it went on for several hours. Before long Lukas thought it was all so exciting that he almost forgot what they were actually doing—looking for his missing cat. Twice he had to run back home for some more water. All the time he was afraid the washing powder would run out, or that somebody would complain that he wasn't cleaning the skateboards well enough. But nobody said anything, and Whirlwind seemed to be pleased. Lukas thought that when he grew up, he might become the world's best skateboard mechanic. No matter how hard he tried, he would never be as good a skateboarder as Whirlwind was.

But Night was still missing.

When they'd finished searching all the gardens and all the other places where he might be hiding, nobody had seen a black cat with a white tip at the end of its tail.

'He's not around here,' said Whirlwind. 'He must be somewhere else.'

Lukas felt a lump in his throat. Night mustn't be a long way away. How would he be able to find his way back home again?

But he didn't say anything.

'That cat will never come back,' said one of Whirlwind's friends. 'You can forget that cat.'

'Hmm,' said Lukas. 'I suppose I'll have to forget about him then.'

It was so very difficult for him to say those words. It was the most difficult thing he'd ever said in the whole of his life. It felt as if Night had heard what he'd said, that Lukas had decided to forget about him. But it wasn't true, of course! He would never forget Night, and he would never stop looking for him. Never ever!

Whirlwind and his friends went off to compete with one another. They were looking for a place where they could make a skateboard track of their own. Lukas went home with his bucket. It almost felt heavier now that it was empty, and he knew that Night hadn't been found today either.

He paused by the currant bush, turned the empty bucket upside down, and sat on it.

He felt sad again now. If only he could understand why Night had run

71

away! Why had he disappeared?

It seemed to Lukas that he would have to do what he'd been thinking of doing for several days. He must run away himself, just like Night did, and go looking for him at night. He must live like a cat in order to be able to find him. As he sat there on the bucket, he started miaowing. He tried to make the same sound as a cat. After a while he became quite good at it. But he wasn't able to purr. The best he could do sounded like Axel when he had a cold and gargled.

Lukas suddenly realised that the next-door neighbour was standing by the fence, staring at him.

'Have you started miaowing, Lukas?' he asked.

'No,' said Lukas. 'I'm only gargling.'

Then he went indoors. The kitchen was empty. Beatrice had gone shopping. Lukas put the bucket and the rag back in the cleaning cupboard.

Then he went to his room and lay down on the bed.

He had no option now.

Tonight, he must run away.

EIGHT

What do you actually do when you want to run away? Lukas didn't know. And so he stayed in his room all afternoon, thinking about what to do.

Children sometimes ran away from home in the books his mum and dad read to him when he was finding it hard to go to sleep. Lukas curled up on the bed and tried to remember everything he'd heard about those children.

What surprised him most was that children always ran away when it was dark outside. How come that children in books are never afraid of the dark? Without hesitation, they all dared to climb out of a window when it was pitch black, and howling gales were lashing the swaying trees. Why wasn't it possible to run away when it was still light? Lukas asked himself. Why couldn't you at least start to run away before the sun had set, and all the shadows had become so scary?

And besides, where would he run away to? In the books his mum and dad read to him, the children were always running away to somewhere in particular. To a parent who lived a long way away beyond a vast, dark forest. Or to a castle on a rock in the middle of a raging ocean. But where would Lukas go to? He didn't know where Night was, after all! It would have been much easier to run away if he'd known where Night was hiding. But then again, if he knew that, he wouldn't need to run away.

Lukas sighed and put the pillow over his face. It was always difficult to do something you'd never done before. Besides, he'd never heard anything about running away being something they taught you in school. Whirlwind had never said anything about lessons in running away studies.

Lukas threw his pillow at the wall in frustration.

He'd decided that he was going to run away and look for Night. But he didn't like the idea of having to do that at all. He fetched the pillow and lay

74

down on his bed again. Then he tried thinking so hard about Night that his cat had no choice but to come back. When he reckoned he'd been thinking hard for long enough, he jumped up and ran over to the window. Night was bound to be sitting out there on the lawn, gazing up at the window.

But the lawn was empty. Apart from a lone magpie, hopping around and pecking between blades of grass.

Maybe that's Night, who's been transformed, Lukas thought. Somebody's turned him into a magpie. He carefully opened the window and shouted for Night—but the magpie was scared and flew off, settling on the chimney of one of the neighbouring houses. Lukas closed the window and sighed again. He tried to sigh so loudly that Night would have to hear him. But all that happened was that Beatrice opened his door and asked if he was ill.

'No,' said Lukas. 'I'm not ill.'

'Are you hungry?' she asked.

Lukas tested. He wasn't really hungry. But if he was going to run away, he needed to eat. He followed his mum into the kitchen.

It was already late afternoon. Lukas heard Whirlwind slamming the front door then rushing into the kitchen to get something from the fridge. Shortly afterwards the front door slammed again. Whirlwind was always in a hurry. It was as if he always needed to whirl around in order to do everything he wanted to do.

Lukas felt a bit jealous, and wished he were the one who whirled around in the world. He didn't like being a Lukas who sat around in his room not knowing what to do in order to run away.

But run away is what he did. Shortly after Axel had come home. He'd made a few sandwiches and put them in his red rucksack. He'd also packed a tin of cat food, his piggy bank containing thirty-two kronor, a compass he'd been given by Whirlwind, and his pillow. He didn't have room for a blanket. But he didn't think he'd be able to leave home without his pillow.

He sneaked out of the front door, climbed over the fence at the back of the house, adjusted his rucksack, took a deep breath, and said aloud to himself: 'Now I've run away!'

He didn't know what to do next. Which direction should he take? Should he head for town, or for the forest? Should he tiptoe along, or walk normally? Could anybody tell by looking at him that he'd run away?

Dusk had slowly started to set in. Dark clouds were hanging over the forest in the far distance.

He decided to walk towards town. Partly because it would probably start raining soon, but also because it was light in the town's streets. He thought that Night surely couldn't be so stupid as to be hiding away in the forest, where Lukas would never be able to find him. Night was a clever cat.

Now and then Lukas would turn round to see if his mum or dad had come looking for him in the car. But there were hardly any cars on the road at all. It was such an unpleasant evening that only those who had run away from home were out in the streets. Lukas thought that all the people he passed, and the ones he saw behind the wheel of the few cars on the road, were running away. Perhaps certain evenings were running away evenings? When only those running away needed to be out and about?

He could see the town lights in the distance. Soon he would come to the dual carriageway that led into town. He wondered if he'd have the strength to walk as far as that? Maybe he'd have to stop and sleep by the roadside?

The thought that he might have to sleep out in the open gave him stomachache. Would he be brave enough to do that? And where would he sleep? He couldn't simply lie down on the pavement. Should he see if he could find one of those places they called hotels? He knew that you could sleep in a hotel if you had enough money. That thought made him feel a bit happier. Besides, he had his own pillow with him. He'd tell the people at the hotel that he only needed a sheet and a duvet. That would make them realise they were dealing with somebody who knew what to do when they were running away.

It was a long way to town. But Lukas kept on walking and walking. He occasionally stopped and looked around, to see if Night was following him. But the only animal he saw was a dog on a lead, with an old lady.

It was dark now, and it had started drizzling. Lukas tried to walk a bit faster, so that he would get to town before it started pouring down. It also occurred to him that his mum and dad must have begun to wonder where he was. He'd normally be in bed by this time. He noticed that he was starting to feel tired.

He eventually came to the edge of town. By then, he was so sleepy that he had to sit down on a bench and rest. He nearly fell asleep on the spot. In order to stay awake, he ate one of the sandwiches he'd taken with him in his rucksack. Then he set off walking again. Now it was light everywhere, from all the shop windows. He suddenly gave a start and stopped dead. In one of the big windows was a big black cat, sitting there and looking at him. When he went to examine it more closely, he saw it was made of porcelain.

That's a clue, he thought. That means that Night is here in town somewhere.

He wanted to know what time it was. He stopped at a hot dog stall and hid in the shadows until there were no customers. Then he went to ask the time. He had to stand on tiptoe in order to see over the counter.

'A quarter to nine,' said a girl chewing gum. 'Do you want a hot dog?'

'No,' said Lukas. 'Thank you very much.'

'Thank you for what?' she said angrily, closing the hatch.

Lukas hurried away. He'd been a bit scared of that girl. Maybe people who lived in the town didn't like people who had run away from home and asked about the time without buying anything?

He started looking for a hotel. If he was going to have enough strength to run further away, he must soon get some sleep. He trudged along street after street, and soon was so tired that he almost burst out crying. He'd never have the strength to walk back home—and besides, he didn't even know how to get there. He'd lost his sense of direction ages ago, wandering from street to street. He started to have nasty thoughts about Night, who'd caused all this trouble by running away from Lukas.

He eventually came to a big square where he could see a building with a large sign saying Hotel. It was a big house with lots of lit-up windows. Music was playing, and lots of people were sitting at tables, eating. He sat down on the steps, took out his piggy bank, opened it and counted up his money. He'd been right, he had thirty-two kronor.

Then he went in through the big doors. The room he'd come into was very large. And full of people rushing back and forth. Somebody was laughing very loudly, somebody else was using a telephone, and speaking a language Lukas didn't understand. A man was standing behind a high counter, handing keys to people who came up to him. Lukas waited until there was nobody waiting there, then he plucked up courage and went there himself. The counter was so high that he could barely reach up to it this time either.

'I want to sleep,' he said to the man with the keys. 'I have my own pillow.'

The man behind the counter didn't hear him. Lukas said it again, but a bit louder. Still the man with the keys didn't hear.

So he shouted.

'I want to sleep. I have my own pillow.'

The man behind the desk gave a start. Then he noticed Lukas.

'What did you say?' he asked.

Lukas said it yet again.

The man eyed him thoughtfully up and down. Then he put his glasses on and leaned over the counter to take a closer look at Lukas.

'How old are you?' he asked.

Lukas thought it was best to be polite.

'I'm seven,' he said. 'My name's

Lukas and I'm looking for my cat. I need to sleep now. I have my own pillow with me. And I have thirty-two kronor. I can pay.'

The man looked serious, and nodded.

'I'm sure you can,' he said. 'I think you'd better come back here with me so that we can talk a bit more about it.'

He opened a little door under the counter and beckoned Lukas into a back room with a bed, a table and a television set.

'So you're out looking for your cat, are you?'

'It's run away,' said Lukas.

'And so you're out tonight, looking for it?'

Lukas thought it might be best to tell him the facts.

'I've run away,' he said. 'If you're going to be able to find a cat that's run away, you have to run away yourself.'

The man nodded.

'I see,' said the man. 'Where do you live when you're not running away?'

'In Rowan Tree Road,' said Lukas.

'You said your name was Lukas. But

when you take a room in a hotel, you have to give your surname as well.'

'Johanson,' said Lukas.

The man nodded, and smiled.

'Of course you can have a room,' said the man. 'Why not lie down on that bed while I fix it for you? You can have something to drink as well, if you're thirsty.'

'I can pay,' said Lukas.

'I'm sure you can,' said the man, taking a bottle of pop from a little refrigerator. 'I won't be a minute.'

Lukas took his pillow out of his rucksack. He was so tired that he could hardly stand up. But he was so proud that he'd proved he could run away.

He lay down on the bed with his head on his own pillow, and looked at the door, which was standing ajar. The man who'd been so kind to him kept looking at him and smiling. He seemed to be leafing through a telephone directory.

Lukas wondered what kind of a room he'd get, and if there would be any toys in it.

That was his last thought before

falling asleep.

He noticed nothing at all when Axel and Beatrice came into the little room, and Axel picked him up and carried him out to the car.

Nor did he hear what the man with the keys said to his mum.

'He must be very fond of his cat,' said the man.

'Yes,' said Beatrice. 'He is very fond of his cat.'

Then they drove back home to Rowan Tree Road.

Lukas didn't notice a thing.

He was fast asleep.

NINE

The next day, when Lukas woke up, it seemed to him as if everything that had happened the previous evening was a dream.

Had he really walked all that way to town? And the man at the hotel—did he really exist, or was he also somebody who vanished the moment Lukas woke up?

But when he went to the kitchen and looked straight into Beatrice's serious eyes, he knew that what had happened last night hadn't been a dream. He recognised that look of hers, and he knew that something serious had happened. It had all taken place in the real world.

But how had he got home? He didn't know. He tried to work out what must have happened. If he really had walked into town, he couldn't simply have dreamed himself back into his own bed?

Or had he been asleep all the way back?

No, he couldn't understand what had happened. Beatrice sighed, but said nothing. And Lukas didn't feel like asking. He was afraid of what she might say.

Lukas ate his breakfast without saying a single word. Then he went back to his room. He didn't know what he would find to do. Nor could he bring himself to think about Night just now. He messed about with his toys and thought about the fact that he'd be starting school soon. How would that go? What if he turned out to be the type who could never learn anything? He felt the need to find out more about that right away. He sat down on the floor with his alarm clock in his hand, and decided that he would learn to tell the time before he started school. If he could teach himself how to do that, he would have proved that he was the type who could learn things.

But he didn't get that far. This was a very odd morning, and to make it even odder he suddenly noticed Axel standing in the doorway, looking at him. Why wasn't he out on the roads with his lorry? Had something happened? Lukas was worried. But Axel merely smiled and sat down on the floor beside him.

'What are you doing, Lukas?' he asked.

'Nothing,' said Lukas. 'I thought I'd try to teach myself how to tell the time.'

'Can't you do that already?' asked Axel in surprise.

'Not properly,' said Lukas. 'I've a bit more to learn yet. The little hand is hardest.'

'I'm with you there,' said Axel. 'The little hand is really hard—it moves so slowly.'

'Why aren't you out in your lorry today?' Lukas eventually got round to asking.

'I've taken the day off,' said Axel. 'I thought you and I could do something together.'

Lukas's heart immediately started racing. This had hardly ever happened before—his dad taking time off work in order to be with Lukas. The only time he'd ever taken a day off before was when Whirlwind had fallen out of a tree and hit his head. But Lukas wasn't ill.

Even so, Dad had taken the day off. Why?

'What shall we do?' Lukas asked.

'I thought we could drive out to the camp site,' said his dad. 'If we put our walking boots on, we can go for a stroll in the forest. We might get to see an elk.'

Axel had hardly finished the sentence before Lukas raced out into the hall and started lacing up his walking boots.

They were soon on their way. They drove through town, past the school that Lukas would soon be attending. It was standing empty at the moment, but the summer holidays would be over before long.

Lukas suddenly realised that his father was watching him through the rear-view mirror. When his eyes met Lukas's, he started to smile. Lukas felt almost embarrassed. He wasn't used to his dad looking at him for no apparent reason.

They turned off from the main road, and the car bumped its way along the rough track towards the lake. Dad wound down the window, and Lukas could smell the scents of the forest.

The camp site was deserted. Caravans were empty and abandoned. Some of them had already been towed away, taken home to stand in the garden or in the garage over the long winter.

Axel walked down to the shore and

gazed out over the lake. Lukas stood beside him, aping him, his legs wide apart and his hands by his sides. Dark clouds were closing in from the edge of the forest on the other side of the lake.

'We live in a rainy-weather land,' said Axel.

'Yes,' said Lukas, who didn't really know how to respond to that. 'It certainly does rain sometimes.'

Lukas could hear that his response sounded odd, as if he were pretending to be grown up. It was a bit like somebody singing out of tune. Grown-ups should sound like grown-ups, and children like children—otherwise, there was something wrong.

'Let's go,' said his dad. 'We'll take that path over there.'

They were soon deep in the forest. They could no longer see the lake, and it was as dark as late afternoon in there among the trees. There was an occasional sound of flapping wings among the tall tree trunks.

'The birds can see us, but we can't see them,' said Axel.

They came to a clearing. It was a bit

lighter there. Dad took off his cap and placed it on a tree stump before sitting down on it. Lukas did the same. That's why we have parents, he thought. So that we know when to take our cap off and put it on a tree stump before sitting down.

'A rainy-weather land,' said Axel again.

Lukas had the impression that Axel wanted to tell him something, but didn't know how to begin.

'I understand how sad you must be because your cat has run away,' said his dad after a while. 'You want him to come back home, of course. But you can't tame cats. They might live with people, but they're still wild. It's a bit hard to explain. Do you understand what I mean?'

'Yes,' said Lukas. Although he hadn't a clue what his dad was saying. How could a cat be wild and tame at the same time? Could people be like that as well? Was it the wild Lukas who had run away the previous evening? And the tame Lukas who was now sitting on a tree stump in the depths of the forest?

'You have to understand that Night is just as happy when he's living out in the wilds,' his dad went on. 'Maybe he was a cat that couldn't be tamed. If we'd forced him to stay at home, it would have been like locking him up in a cage.'

Axel scratched away at the back of his neck before continuing solemnly.

'I thought it would be best if we had a little chat about this, just you and me,' he said. 'Your mum and I are a bit worried about you thinking about Night all the time.'

'I want him to come back,' said Lukas, and could feel the lump in his throat.

'Maybe it's better for him to be living wild in a rainy-weather land,' said Dad.

'Cats don't like rain,' said Lukas.

'But Night ran away when it was pouring down,' said his dad. 'Perhaps Night is an unusual cat who likes bad weather.'

Lukas needed to think about that. Maybe his dad was right? Maybe Night was the only cat in the world who liked rain? But in that case, where is this special rainy-weather land?

He asked his dad.

'Nobody really knows where it is,' said Axel. 'But what I do know is that all the cats who live there put umbrellas up when it's sunny and they sit outside in their gardens, and they are happiest when it's raining. The raindrops are warm, and they give you a tan. Sometimes the rain is so warm that they have to find a place where the sun is shining so that they can find some shade and feel cool.'

'That's a very strange country,' said Lukas. 'Is it on the map?'

'No,' said his dad. 'Only the very best and most remarkable cats ever find their way there. They don't need maps. They follow the rain clouds, and they eventually get there.'

'Is there food for them in that country?' Lukas wondered.

'There's everything a cat could possibly want there,' said Axel. 'Cats couldn't possibly find anywhere better to live than the rainy-weather land.'

Lukas didn't really know what to

believe. Obviously, what his dad was saying was a fairy tale—but it was a lovely fairy tale. It was easier to think about Night after having heard Dad talking about this strange country far, far away, where it rained all the time.

'That's why I took the day off,' said Axel. 'So that we could come out here into the forest and talk about Night.'

'Will Night ever come back?' Lukas asked.

'Possibly not,' said his dad. 'But I'm quite sure that he's thinking about you just as much as you're thinking about him.'

'Can't we go and visit him?' Lukas asked.

'Where?'

'In the rainy-weather land.'

'There's no way we could go there, neither walking or by car,' said his dad.

'How did Night get there, then?'

There was a long pause before Axel answered. Lukas had the feeling that his dad didn't really know.

'Cats have remarkable eyes,' he said in the end. 'They can see much better than we can when it's dark. Sometimes, when it rains at night, really big drops fall to the ground—as big as beach balls. Cats who want to go to the rainy-weather land creep inside those enormous drops. Then they start spinning round at tremendous speed and woosh!—They vanish; and when they've vanished they are there.'

Lukas didn't know what to think. What his dad had told him sounded exciting—but could it really be true? Did raindrops as big as that really fall during the night?

'I want Night to come back even so,' said Lukas. 'Even if he can only come to say hello now and again. Maybe it's possible to write letters to that strange land?'

'We'll have to see if we can find out the address,' said Axel, standing up. 'Maybe all we need to do is to leave a letter under that wild currant bush where he used to lie and sleep? Maybe the cats have a secret postman who collects such letters?'

Lukas decided that he would write a letter to Night as soon as he'd learnt how to write and spell at school. Now he wanted to start school immediately.

'I'll write letters to him,' said Lukas. 'I'll write every single day.'

They walked back through the forest. Lukas held his dad's hand. When they got back to the lake shore, Lukas remembered something.

'We didn't see an elk,' he said.

'But perhaps there was an elk who saw us,' said his dad.

Then they drove home.

That evening Lukas placed an envelope containing a photograph of himself under the currant bush. He thought it would be best for Night to have a picture so that he wouldn't forget what Lukas looked like.

His mum had helped him to address the envelope.

To:
Night the Cat,
Rainy-Weather Land.

The next morning it was still there under the bush.

But Lukas wasn't going to give up. Sooner or later the cats' secret postman would come and collect his letter. He was absolutely certain of that.

TEN

It suddenly occurred to Lukas that he had almost stopped laughing.

How on earth could that be possible? He was always so cheerful, and could laugh at anything you like.

Obviously, it was because Night hadn't come back. Lukas thought days were long, and hard to get through—as if every hour was a heavy boot with lots of mud clinging to its sole.

One morning he woke up feeling bitter and angry, and went to join his mum in the kitchen.

'Good morning, Lukas,' she said. 'Did you sleep well?'

'No,' said Lukas. 'I slept bloody awful.'

'You mustn't speak like that,' said his mother sternly.

'I slept bloody awful,' said Lukas

again, but even louder this time, as if he wanted everybody in Rowan Tree Road to hear him.

'What's the matter with you?' Beatrice wondered.

'I'm not going to start school,' said Lukas.

'Of course you're going to start school,' she said. 'You've been looking forward to it for so long now.'

'I can't start school as long as Night is missing. How would I be able to look for him?'

'I can keep an eye on the road while you're in school.'

Lukas didn't think much of that. It wasn't enough simply to wander over to a window now and then and take a look at the road or the garden.

If you were going to find a cat that had run away, you would have to spend all your time searching and looking out of the window.

'Anyway, I'm not going to start school,' said Lukas, and stormed out of the kitchen. He wondered if he ought to slam the door behind him, but he didn't dare. His mum could sometimes get very angry—so angry that Lukas was sort of scared.

'Aren't you going to have any breakfast?' asked Beatrice in surprise.

'I'm not hungry,' said Lukas. 'Do we really have to spend all our time eating?'

Lukas got dressed and went out. There was a nip in the air, and he shivered as he trudged through the garden towards the fence. He looked round. None of his friends were out. The only living thing apart from himself was a magpie, wagging its tail up and down on a fence not far away.

Lukas went to the wild currant bush.

He stopped dead.

The letter! He'd forgotten all about the letter. And now it had vanished. There was nothing under the currant bush.

Somebody had been there and collected his letter.

He stared at the ground where the envelope had been lying underneath a lump of granite. No, his eyes weren't deceiving him. Somebody had been there during the night, and fetched it.

It was on its way to Rainy-Weather Land. Night would soon be holding it in his paws.

Lukas burst out laughing. There was a bubbling inside him, as if he was about to belch. And then the laughter came tumbling out, like a balloon of bubble-gum bursting. Nobody could laugh like Lukas, when he was really happy. It sounded like trumpets and neighing horses and clattering magpies.

The curious neighbour, who always seemed to be standing by his fence and keeping an eye on Lukas, couldn't resist asking what was so funny. But Lukas didn't reply. He just carried on laughing. He knew now that Night was safe and sound.

He still didn't understand why Night had run away. But perhaps he'd get a reply from him? Perhaps Night was so remarkable that he could transform his miaows into a sort of words that Lukas would be able to understand. Maybe Night would be able to hold a pen in his paw and write letters. Why not? Were there any limits to what that remarkable cat could do?

Lukas decided on the spot to go home and write another letter. Maybe the secret postman would come back again tonight as well? He felt an urge to tell his mum what had happened. She would have to help him to write the next letter.

Now he could start thinking seriously about starting school, despite everything. It didn't feel so bad, now that he knew Night would soon receive his greeting. He'd soon be sitting with the photograph of Lukas in his paws. Maybe he'd even regret having run away? Lukas wondered if it might be possible for him to create a sort of mini rainy-weather land for Night in his room. If he hung a watering can from the ceiling, it could create showers to fall on Night. Would that be enough?

He started running towards the gate. He was in a hurry. There was so much he needed to do! Now! Straight away!

Just as he was opening the gate, Whirlwind came speeding up on his skateboard. He had some of his friends with him.

'Have you found the cat?' Whirlwind

shouted.

'No,' said Lukas. He didn't want to tell him how he'd sent a letter to Rainy-Weather Land. Whirlwind and his friends might think that was a childish thing to do, and start asking awkward questions. It was best to say nothing at all.

'We're going to start building a skateboard track now,' said Whirlwind. 'Guess where it's going to be!'

Lukas only liked guessing when he was sure he was right. But he had no idea where Whirlwind and his friends were going to build their track. So he said nothing.

'There,' said Whirlwind, pointing.

Lukas followed the direction indicated by Whirlwind's finger—and had a terrible shock.

Whirlwind was pointing straight at the old currant bush.

'It's a good place,' said Whirlwind. 'We'll pull down that old bush. Then we can build our track.'

'But you can't,' said Lukas, and he felt a lump in his throat, growing bigger and bigger.

'Why can't we?' asked Whirlwind. 'Just wait and see. We're off now to get some of the wood we need for making the track.'

And they raced away.

Lukas stared after them. Now all his joy had vanished again. Why did they have to build their track in the very place where the currant bush was standing? Surely that wasn't possible? It was Night's place, and nobody was allowed to touch it.

Lukas didn't know what to do next. How could he explain to Whirlwind that they would have to build their track somewhere else?

What should he do? How could he defend his currant bush. All by himself? Night would never come back if the currant bush was no longer there.

He tried to think of a solution. The currant bush was wild. That must mean that nobody owned it. Maybe he could buy it for the thirty-two kronor he'd saved up. But who should he pay if nobody owned the bush? Could you say that it was Night's bush because he was the only one who used it? But Night was missing, of course. And Night was only a cat. No, that was no good. He must think of something else.

He walked slowly over to the currant bush. There were only a few dried up, half-rotten currants left, on the end of one of the branches.

'It's not possible,' he said to himself. 'Whirlwind can't be allowed to pull down the currant bush. If he does, Night will never come back.'

Although it was damp on the ground, Lukas sat down. How would he be able to defend the currant bush? When he was on his own, and up against all Whirlwind's gang?

Dad, he thought. He'll understand. He'll have to help me. We've been out in the forest together, and talked. He knows what it's like to love a cat more than anything else in the world.

Lukas stood up and went indoors.

'Do you still not want any breakfast?' asked his mother.

'I'm not hungry,' said Lukas.

It wasn't true. He was hungry. But he didn't think it was right to eat when somebody was going to destroy Night's currant bush.

'Are you ill?' his mum wondered.

'No,' said Lukas. 'I just want to be left alone.'

Beatrice looked hard at him, but she didn't say anything. She left him alone with his thoughts.

Lukas sat down on a chair by the window and looked out. He hadn't bothered to take his boots off. There was a pool of dirty water on the floor, but he didn't care.

I hope it takes a long time, he thought. I hope it takes ages and ages for Whirlwind and his friends to collect all the wood they need for the skateboard track. I hope they don't have enough money to pay for it all. I hope, hope, hope . . . But most of all he hoped that they wouldn't have time to dig up the bush before his dad came home for his evening meal.

Lukas was so nervous that he had stomachache. He couldn't sit still on the chair any longer, and went to the kitchen.

'Is Dad coming home for dinner tonight?' he asked his mum.

'Haven't you taken your boots off?' she said. 'Look, there's dirt all over the floor!'

'Is Dad coming home for dinner?' Lukas asked again.

Beatrice looked at him and frowned. Lukas couldn't tell if she was angry or worried.

'What's the matter with you?' she wondered.

'Nothing,' said Lukas. 'I just want to know if Dad's coming home for dinner tonight.'

'He's coming home for dinner as usual,' said Beatrice. 'Why ever shouldn't he?'

'I don't know,' said Lukas. 'But I need to talk to him.'

'Can't you talk to me just as well?'

'No,' said Lukas. 'Only Dad understands this.'

To avoid having to answer any more questions, he went back to the chair by the window. But first he took his boots off in the hall.

Whirlwind and his friends still hadn't come back. But there was a long time to go before his dad would drive his lorry back home for dinner.

Would he get back in time?

Lukas waited. And waited. And waited.

Nothing happened. He occasionally went to ask his mum what time it was.

Nothing happened.

Then everything happened all at once.

First, Lukas saw to his horror that Whirlwind and his friends had arrived, pulling a barrow laden with planks of wood. Then he saw his dad's lorry approaching from the other direction. He shouted out loud and jumped up from the chair. Then he ran out into the garden to welcome his dad. He forgot to put his boots on. But all that mattered was the currant bush. Would his dad understand that it had to stay? Or would Whirlwind get permission to pull it down?

ELEVEN

Sometimes, Lukas simply couldn't understand how he'd had the courage to do what he had done. Like now, when he ran through the garden in his stockinged feet then started jumping up and down and flailing with his arms in front of his dad, who had stopped dead in astonishment. Lukas tried to explain what was happening, but he was in such a hurry that he mixed everything up. The words whirred round and round inside his mouth and came tumbling out in the wrong order. He could see that his dad hadn't a clue what was going on. That only made Lukas all the more excited. He started again from the beginning, but Axel merely shook his head.

'I don't know what you're on about,' he said. 'And why are you running around the garden with no shoes on? What do you think your mum would say if she saw you?'

'Whirlwind is going to cut down the

currant bush,' Lukas yelled. 'But he can't, because it's Night's. How will Night be able to find his way home if the currant bush isn't there any longer? They'll have to build their track somewhere else.'

'Calm down now,' said Axel. 'What track?'

'The currant bush,' yelled Lukas again. 'The currant bush, the currant bush . . .'

He shouted so loudly that Whirlwind and his friends heard what he was saying. Whirlwind immediately came storming in through the garden gate and joined in the discussions. He and Lukas started shouting at each other, and Axel understood even less of what they were saying. By now, Beatrice had begun to wonder what all the yelling in the garden was about. When she looked out of the door, the first thing she noticed was that Lukas had no shoes on.

'Come in this minute!' she cried.

Lukas heard what she said, but he couldn't answer—he had no time to put shoes on. Besides, he didn't have any words left. His mouth was completely empty. There was nothing left to come out, not even a squeak.

Then Lukas did something he'd never dared to do before. He didn't dare now either, but he did it even so. He attacked Whirlwind and started punching him. Naturally enough, Whirlwind was angry and was just about to start hitting back when Axel grabbed hold of his arm. Beatrice came running up and took hold of Lukas, who was preparing to attack Whirlwind again. It was absolute chaos. Whirlwind's friends thought it was best to keep out of it, and they lost no time in hastening away on their skateboards. The neighbours were fascinated by what was going on, and were lined up along the fences, taking it all in.

'That's enough of all this nonsense,' Axel roared. 'What on earth's going on?'

'I don't know,' said Beatrice.

'Lukas is an idiot,' yelled Whirlwind, in a temper.

'That's enough, now,' said Axel.

'You're the one who's an idiot!'

yelled Lukas at Whirlwind.

'Shut up, the pair of you,' roared Axel.

He was really angry now. He dragged Whirlwind and Lukas in through the front door and slammed it behind them.

'You mustn't go out in your stockinged feet,' said Beatrice again. 'You'll catch your death of cold.'

Lukas said nothing. He just stared at his mother's feet. She had also forgotten to put her shoes on before running out. But he made no comment. The only thing that mattered was the currant bush.

'So, let's sit down in the kitchen and sort all this out,' said Axel. 'Everybody.'

'Me first,' said Whirlwind.

'I was first,' said Lukas.

'I'm oldest,' said Whirlwind.

'I'm youngest,' said Lukas.

Axel sighed and sat down at the kitchen table.

'I suppose I'd better start things going,' he said. 'And I think Lukas had better speak first—but not because he was the one shouting loudest.'

Lukas gave Whirlwind a self-satisfied smile. He explained to his dad why he didn't want Axel and his friends to build a skateboard track where the currant bush was standing. Words were no longer jumping around in his mouth. They came out in the right order.

Then it was Whirlwind's turn. He glared angrily at Lukas.

'Everything's become a problem since that cat vanished,' he said. 'It was bad enough when it arrived. Then it became a problem when it went missing. I hope it never comes back.'

Lukas roared like a lion and hurled himself at Whirlwind. It happened so quickly that neither Axel nor Beatrice was able to stop him. The chair Whirlwind was sitting on was overturned, and the pair of them landed on the floor. Then Lukas felt his father's fist grabbing hold of the back of his collar. He was picked up and returned to his chair.

Lukas was afraid that his dad was now so angry that he wouldn't want to hear another single word about cats or currant bushes. But he was wrong.

Instead of ranting and raving, Axel burst out laughing.

'That cat has bewitched us,' he said. 'I think it's sitting back somewhere and laughing its head off at us.'

'But it's not sitting under the currant bush, that's for sure,' said Whirlwind.

'Night can make himself invisible when he wants to,' said Lukas.

Axel stood up.

'Let's go out and take a closer look at that currant bush,' he said. 'Maybe you can build your skateboard track without needing to dig up the currant bush?'

'That's not possible,' said Whirlwind.

'Of course it is,' said Lukas.

'How?' wondered Whirlwind, far from pleased.

Lukas couldn't answer that. He was afraid that his dad wouldn't be able to solve the problem.

But he could. They went out and took a closer look at the currant bush. Whirlwind started by explaining what their plans were. His dad thought for a moment, then said:

'But why don't you build your track over the top of the currant bush? You could make it a sort of roof.'

Whirlwind was about to protest when Axel went on:

'That would mean that the currant bush was untouched, but you'd still have your track. And Lukas can help you to build it. That's only fair.'

'He'd only get in the way,' said Whirlwind angrily.

'But surely he could hold the planks and keep them steady while you do the sawing,' said Axel.

'I want a dog,' said Whirlwind out of the blue. 'A big dog. That barks whenever anybody says "Lukas".'

'You can't have a dog and a cat in the same house,' said Lukas.

'I think you can,' said Axel. 'But we'd better hold back for a while before getting any more pets. What we must do first is wait and see if Night comes back.'

'He will come back,' said Lukas firmly.

'Yes, yes,' said Axel. 'Perhaps he will. But now it's time to go and eat. And I don't want any more arguing.'

Then Whirlwind and his friends built their skateboard track, and Lukas was with them although he wasn't really allowed to help. It took almost a whole week, and most probably the track would never have been finished if Axel hadn't lent a hand in the evenings.

But there it was in the end, and the currant bush had got its roof. Lukas could crawl underneath the track and hear the swishing of the skateboards passing over his head. He'd even be able to sit there and wait for Night when it was raining.

But Night didn't come back. And the day when Lukas would start school was coming closer and closer. Every afternoon, he would nag away at his mum until she helped him to write another letter to Night. Then he would place it under the currant bush, and the following morning it would have vanished. Deep down he knew that there wasn't a postman collecting his letters. You couldn't be so childish as to believe that when you'd soon be starting school. Perhaps the letters simply blew away during the night. Perhaps there was some strange animal that came out at night and enjoyed eating paper.

Lukas tried harder and harder to think the unpleasant thought that in fact, Night would never come back. He was missing, and would always be missing. And Lukas would never find out why he'd run away. Night had become a riddle that would never be solved.

One day, just before Lukas was due to start school, he made his first attempt to get help in finding Night. He'd gone to town with his mum when she went shopping. He'd taken with him all the thirty-two kronor he'd saved, but he didn't say what he was intending to do with it.

Next to the big shopping mall where Beatrice would spend at least an hour was a park with a children's playground. He'd been allowed to go there on his own before, while his mum did the shopping. He promised not to run away, and hurried to the big park.

But he wasn't actually going to the

116

playground.

He knew that there was a fountain in the park, known as the wishing well. People who wanted a wish to come true would throw money into the water. His dad had often said that it was sheer madness, throwing money into the well. But Lukas had decided that he had nothing to lose. He believed that somehow or other, Night would discover that Lukas had thrown all his money into the water. And then he would have to come back.

He was out of breath by the time he reached the fountain. It was in the form of a big fish squirting lots of water straight up into the air.

As he had some paper notes as well as coins, Lukas had taken his secret piggy bank with him. So that the notes wouldn't blow away, or just float on the surface of the water, he'd decided to throw in the whole lot: then he could be sure it would sink to the bottom.

He was the only one by the fountain. He knew that when you threw in your money, all you should be thinking about was the wish you wanted to come true. Otherwise nothing would happen.

But as he was thinking so hard that he closed his eyes, he couldn't keep his balance when he threw the piggy bank into the well. He fell into the water and got soaking wet through.

It wasn't very deep, but the water was freezing cold and he started shivering. He couldn't see any sign of the piggy bank, no matter how hard he looked into the bubbling water.

Then his teeth began chattering, and he ran through the park in his dripping wet clothes. He didn't wait by the car, but ran straight into the supermarket, and eventually found his mum in among the shelves. She stared at him in horror.

'You're wet through!' she said. 'What have you been doing?'

'It's a secret,' Lukas told her. 'Some secrets can make you wet.'

Lukas couldn't understand why, but Beatrice didn't ask him any more questions. Perhaps she suspected it had something to do with Night.

She left the trolley and its contents where it was, and drove him home so that he could put some dry clothes on.

'I expect it's true that some secrets can make you wet,' she said. 'But no more wet secrets today, all right?'

'I promise,' said Lukas.

Then Beatrice drove back to the mall to finish her shopping.

Lukas sat by the window, looking for Night.

But he didn't come back that day either, even though Lukas had almost sacrificed himself in the wishing well.

Now there was only one thing he could do.

Wait. And wait. And wait.

TWELVE

The night before Lukas started school, he had a remarkable dream. At first he'd found it difficult to get to sleep. His mum had sat on the edge of his bed and read aloud several stories that Lukas liked to hear. But she'd also told him he needn't feel nervous about his first day at school. He'd been to meet the teacher some time ago, and he knew several of the children who would be starting at the same time and in the same class.

'I'm not frightened,' said Lukas.

'Good!' said Beatrice. 'Sleep well!'

She left a lamp on and closed the door quietly. Lukas could hear the sound of the television in the background, and that was when the remarkable dream started, even before he fell asleep.

He was lying and looking at the lampshade, the faint light behind the thick red shade. Suddenly, he had the impression that everything was becoming lighter. Stars seemed to be glittering from the ceiling. Just next to the old cupboard with his old teddy bear on top, a pale half-moon was shining, exactly as if the moon had sunk down from the sky and somehow smuggled its way in through the closed window. A campfire was burning in the middle of the floor. Shadows danced along the walls, and Lukas thought it was an interesting dream—but he wasn't asleep.

Just for a moment he felt afraid, and pulled the sheet over his head. But when he smelled the smoke from the campfire in his nostrils, he pulled it down again and decided that it wasn't a dangerous dream, just something unusual and remarkable.

He sat up in bed.

Yes, the whole room had changed. He noticed that the curtains now looked like a door. He got out of bed, was careful not to go too near the fire, and made his way to the window.

When he carefully opened the curtains, he saw that the window behind them really had changed into a door.

He tried the handle and opened the door. There was no longer a garden outside. There were no other houses, and no Rowan Tree Road. There was something else. Something remarkable . . .

He went back to his bed and sat down on the edge of it. Then he noticed something yellow lying next to the campfire. He couldn't see what it was at first, but when he leaned forward he saw it was Night's collar. The one he'd been wearing the day he wandered off to Rainy-Weather Land.

He noticed that his heart was pounding. Night was somewhere close by. He went back to the window.

It was totally dark outside, because the moon and the stars were inside his room. But then he realised that he could see even so. Just like Night, he thought. In this strange dream I can see in the dark just as well as Night.

Then he heard a sound coming from the darkness. He knew immediately what it was. His ears had become just as good as Night's as well.

But was it really Night miaowing in the darkness?

He thought he could glimpse something black, but he wasn't sure. He held his breath and waited. Then he heard the sound again.

Night, Lukas thought. You've come back after all. You're coming to greet me, even though it is only in a strange dream.

There was a ladder leaning against the window that had changed into a door. Lukas clambered out onto the ladder.

Although it was cold outside, he didn't feel cold. I've probably got thick fur now as well, even if it is invisible, he thought. Every time he put his foot on a new rung, he could hear various tunes playing for him.

When he stepped onto the last rung of all, he could hear the tune he liked best of all, *Silent Night*. And he remembered singing it to Night, one of the last days just before he vanished.

When he reached the ground, he noticed that it was drizzling slightly. But he didn't get wet at all, and the rain was warm—it was like standing under a warm shower.

I'm in Rainy-Weather Land, he thought. When Night realised that I wouldn't be able to find my way there, he came to me and brought the land with him in a dream instead.

He could hear some more miaowing, further away this time. Lukas followed, trying to be as quiet as possible and not to walk on dry, rustling leaves. He listened to the warm rain, and it

123

sounded to him like various tunes. The drops were playing melodies for him, and it was nearly as beautiful as when his mum used to sing to herself.

He suddenly stopped dead. What if he liked Rainy-Weather Land so much that he didn't want to go back home? What if he would never go to school, neither tomorrow nor any other day?

He turned round, frightened of losing his way. He could see the open door of his room, shining brightly through the darkness, high above the ladder. The moonlight shone down in a beam that ended at his feet. If he followed that moonbeam, he'd never find his way back home, he thought.

He heard more miaowing, and followed it. There were no houses at all, only bare ground and some small, odd-looking bushes that all looked the same. Then he realised what they were. Umbrellas. Planted umbrellas. Obviously, nobody needed umbrellas in Rainy-Weather Land. They were allowed to grow wherever they liked, and nobody paid any attention to them.

He suddenly stood still. He didn't

know why, only that he had to stand absolutely still. There was something close by. He pricked up his ears and listened, looking round in the blackness all the while.

That was when he caught sight of Night. He was sitting on top of a massive rock washing his fur with slow movements of his tongue. When Lukas saw him, he turned his head and looked Lukas straight in the eye. It was as if lights had been switched on, connecting their eyes—two beams of light linking their faces like telephone wires.

Night miaowed and raised his tail. Lukas stood perfectly still and realised that he had tears in his eyes. But he forced himself not to burst out crying. He was afraid the tears would extinguish the beams of light between himself and Night.

He stretched up as far as he could. He could nearly reach Night. But only nearly. He couldn't quite reach up to stroke him.

'Jump down,' he whispered. 'Jump down here to me.'

'I can't,' said Night.

'Then I'll climb up to you.'

Night's eyes were extremely serious.

'I'd like you to do that,' he said. 'But if you climb up here, you'll never be able to climb down again. You'll have to stay here in Rainy-Weather Land for ever.'

'That's what I'd like to do,' shouted Lukas. 'I don't want to start school, I don't want to go back to my bed. I want to stay here with you.'

'I know,' said Night. 'But you must stay there with all the humans. You can't live here among the cats.'

'Then you must come back to me,' said Lukas. 'Cats can live with humans.'

Night nodded slowly.

'I'll come back to you,' he said. 'I'll come back in this dream. That's where we can meet.'

'That's not good enough,' shouted Lukas—and now he was quite desperate. 'I want you to be with me always. Why did you leave me? What did I do wrong?'

'You didn't do anything wrong,' said Night. 'You loved me so much that I dared to go off on my own. I know you are always thinking of me. That's what gives me the strength to be a cat that goes to the Rainy-Weather Land.'

'What is it that's so good about being here?' Lukas asked. 'What is it that's so much better here than in Rowan Tree Road?'

'I don't know,' said Night. 'I don't know yet. I just felt that I had to go. You'll have that feeling yourself one of these days. Something you have to do, but don't dare. Then you can think of me.'

'I don't understand,' said Lukas. 'It's too hard to follow.'

'You'll understand one day,' said Night. 'All this is really about you. It's not about me. I'm just a cat who's run away. I want you to be happy when you think about me, even though I have run away. I want you to long for me. Not to miss me.'

Night reached out with a paw. For a split second Lukas was able to feel its soft pad.

Then Night vanished. Lukas ran back to the moonbeam, climbed up the ladder and snuggled down in bed again.

The starry sky on his ceiling slowly faded away, and the moon disappeared through the window once more, the campfire went out, and soon only the night lamp was still shining.

Lukas closed his eyes and tried to return to his dream.

But he simply slept, and didn't wake up until his mum came in the next morning.

Everything that had happened came back to him immediately.

'Can you smell burning?' he asked. Beatrice looked at him in surprise.

'What could have caused a smell of burning?'

'A campfire,' said Lukas.

Beatrice smiled at him.

'You must have been dreaming,' she said. 'Have you forgotten that you start school today?'

'No,' said Lukas as he jumped out of bed and went to the window. Everything was back to usual outside. The houses and the road and the garden. The lone currant bush was crouching on the other side of the fence.

'You can tell me about your dream while we're having breakfast,' said Beatrice.

'There's nothing to tell,' said Lukas. 'It was all so very odd.'

When his mum had left the room, he sat down on his bed.

Before he started getting dressed, he wanted to think through that dream one more time. And as he sat there on the edge of his bed, he had the feeling that he understood what Night had been trying to tell him.

He knew that one of the first days, his teacher would ask everybody in the class to tell the rest about something exciting or funny they'd experienced.

He knew now.

He would tell them about the remarkable cat called Night.

His story would be the most remarkable of all.

THIRTEEN

It was clear to Lukas from the very first day that going to school was going to be fun. The thought that going to school for at least ten more years, nearly twice as long as he'd already lived, every day in the autumn, winter and spring, didn't worry him in the least. He had the impression that life was really, really long. It was like a road that never came to an end.

His mum had accompanied him to school that first day. Lukas would have preferred it if his dad had been there as well, but Axel couldn't take the day off work.

'You can tell me all about it this evening,' he'd said to Lukas. 'I can hardly remember what it was like, starting school. But I might remember when you tell me how you got on.'

There was a chilly breeze, but the sun was shining on the day Lukas started school. As they passed through the garden gate, Lukas took a look at the skateboard track and the wild currant bush. But Night wasn't there.

In fact, Lukas would have been surprised if he'd seen the tip of Night's tail. After all, he knew that Night was in the strange land where umbrellas grow wild.

It seemed to him that Night was a clever cat. He hadn't wanted Lukas to start school and at the same time be worried about what had happened to his missing cat.

As they walked to school, he wondered if, after all, it had been the piggy bank he'd thrown into the wishing well that had made Night come to visit him in that remarkable dream. He would have liked to ask his mum about it. But he'd told her that the wet secret was secret! He couldn't tell anybody about the wishing well. Not yet, at least. If you'd managed to keep a secret for a few days, then maybe it didn't matter so much if you told your mum about it—only her, mind you.

Then they came to the school, and Lukas couldn't continue thinking about Night. It was exciting, starting school.

Lukas knew that you only did it once in your life. And anything you only did once was important, something you would always want to remember. Not forget about it, as his dad had done.

'Do you remember when you started school?' he asked his mum.

'Everybody remembers that,' she said with a smile. 'Except your dad, of course.'

'Was it a long time ago?' Lukas asked.

'Yes,' she sighed. 'Far too long.'

'How long?'

'More than twenty-five years ago.'

Lukas couldn't really imagine how long twenty-five years was. But then, it was good to know that time didn't pass too quickly. That there was room to sleep and play and go to school. And think about your missing cat.

A thought suddenly struck him.

'How old can a cat become?' he asked.

'I don't know,' said Beatrice. 'Pretty old, I think.'

'But how old?'

'Twenty, perhaps.'

'Not twenty-five?'

'Yes,' said Beatrice eventually. 'I think there are probably cats who live to be twenty-five.'

Lukas giggled at the thought of Night growing so old that he needed to walk with the aid of a stick. How would that be possible? Would he need four walking sticks as he had four paws?

But he hadn't time to think that thought to its conclusion. It was time to go to the classroom for real, the first time ever.

He was starting school now.

As early as that first day, their teacher told them all to go home and think about something interesting they'd like to tell their classmates about.

'I'm going to tell them about Night,' Lukas told Beatrice as they walked home together after the first day at school, which had been very short.

She frowned and looked hard at him.

'But that wouldn't be much fun,' she said. 'Telling everybody that you have a cat who's run away. And made you so very sad.'

'I'm not sad any more,' said Lukas.

Beatrice paused.

'You're not? How come?'

'I know that Night is doing fine,' Lukas explained.

'You mean you've seen him?' she asked in surprise. 'You haven't said anything about that.'

'I've dreamt about him,' said Lukas. 'And he's doing fine. He's just gone away. To another land. But I can't tell you any more. The rest is a secret.'

'That's great news,' said Beatrice. 'Your dad will be pleased when he hears that. And Whirlwind as well.'

'Not Whirlwind,' said Lukas sternly. 'He mustn't know anything about that. If I say that Night has gone away, he'll want a dog.'

'Good God, no!' said Beatrice. 'No more animals in the house!'

'No,' said Lukas. 'It's enough with Night. He still lives with us. Even if he is away.'

*   *   *

During the afternoon Lukas crept

under the skateboard track and sat down. He needed to work out how he was going to tell the story of Night to his classmates. It wasn't all that easy. In fact, it was quite difficult to turn it into a story that hung together. Especially as it was about a cat as remarkable as Night.

But in the end, while he was still sitting under the skateboard track and it was starting to get cold, he hit upon the best way of telling it. Now he knew!

When his dad came home in his lorry, Lukas ran out to greet him.

'Now I'm going to tell you what it's like, starting school!' he shouted.

Axel smiled.

'I like it when you come running to meet me, looking happy,' said Axel.

Lukas sniffed at his overall. It smelled of farmyard.

'You've driven to the slaughterhouse today,' said Lukas.

Axel nodded.

Lukas had guessed right!

*   *   *

Two days later, Lukas told the story of Night. He had taken with him all the photographs he had of Night, and shown them to his classmates. He told them all about Night, everything Night had said in that strange dream. He had realised that Night had come back to him in the dream for that very reason: he wanted to give Lukas the most remarkable story of all. He'd wanted to give Lukas something really special and exciting to tell.

Mind you, he wasn't sure afterwards that his classmates had grasped just how remarkable Night actually was. He thought it best to continue talking about Night, even during the breaks. Some of his classmates told him they were sick of hearing about that missing cat. When that happened, Lukas could be angry and sad. But he continued telling everybody about Night even so.

And so, one day, Lukas got a nickname.

Just how it happened, nobody knew.

But suddenly, there it was.

Somebody had said it, and somebody had overheard it and passed it on. You never really know with nicknames. They have their secrets, just as cats can have secrets, and humans as well, come to that.

$$*\qquad *\qquad *$$

You can never be completely sure about where a nickname comes from. Perhaps it was Night himself who'd used it for the first time. Whispered it into the wind that had blown it into the schoolyard, where somebody had heard it, and passed it on.

It was impossible to know.

But one day, somebody in the school yard shouted:

'Lucky Night!'

And Lukas turned round immediately, because he knew he was the one somebody was shouting to.

Lucky Night. Lucky Night.

It sounded odd at first, almost like a foreign language. But soon, everybody had grown used to it, and nobody apart from the teacher called him Lukas any more.

Lucky Night. Lucky Night.

It was a big day in Lukas's life when he got a nickname. Whirlwind was no longer the only one in the family with a nickname. There were two of them now.

'It's a strange nickname,' said Whirlwind. 'But it's a good one. There's nothing else like it.'

'There's nothing else like my cat, either,' said Lukas.

'Oh, come on,' said Whirlwind in irritation. 'It's run away! Stop talking about that cat! Learn how to skateboard instead. Nobody wants to hear about that stupid cat!'

Lukas didn't bother to respond. Earlier, he would no doubt have been both angry and sad. But what does anybody called Lucky Night care about what an elder brother thinks? An elder brother who doesn't even know that the most remarkable cat in the world is now in a land where umbrellas grow wild.

They don't care at all, Lukas thought. I'm not going to stop talking about Night. And if nobody wants to listen, I can always talk to myself. Nobody's going to take my cat away from me.

And soon it was winter, and the skateboard track and the currant bush were both covered in snow. Occasionally cat paw-marks were visible in the white snow. But Lukas knew they were tracks left by another cat. Night was in a land where it rained all the time, a warm rain that sang tunes. Night was sitting there on his rock, licking his fur clean and thinking.

His cat was a king in Rainy-Weather Land.

His rock was his throne. From there he could keep an eye on his enormous realm. Only when it suited him did he receive visits from other cats. On very special occasions, Night would go off with his dream in order to talk to Lukas.

And then the whole world held its breath.

Nobody was allowed to disturb them when Night and Lucky Night were together.

Never, ever . . .

FOURTEEN

And then?

What happened next?

Night never came back. He had vanished forever in the wonderful Rainy-Weather Land that Lukas dreamed about all the time.

Whenever it was cloudy and rain was pattering on the windows, Lukas would stand by his window, his nose pressed up against the pane, and try to see Night. Sometimes he thought the patterns made by the raindrops on the window reminded him of Night's face. Some trickles would suddenly look like whiskers, and two shiny drops could have been Night's eyes. Oh yes, Lukas could see his cat in the rain, and he was happy to think that he had the only cat in the world who liked rain. He'd loved rain so much that he was now in a land where it rained all the time: the secret Rainy-Weather Land that was beyond all roads, all mountains and all seas.

But naturally, Lukas hoped that one

day Night would come back and jump up and lie down next to him on his pillow. He would sleep for a whole day and a whole night, and then he would tell Lukas all about the many adventures he'd had.

But Night didn't come back. Soon, several days could go by without Lukas thinking about Night at all. Then Lukas would be worried in case he forgot all about him. And so he wrote a note that he stuck up on the inside of his door, reminding him to think about Night every single day, for at least five minutes.

Lukas got more and more school work to do. When he thought about Night, it seemed that he was beginning to see him from a distance. At first, soon after Night had disappeared, he had always seemed to be very close by. But now it was almost as if Lukas saw him as a little black dot, far, far away.

*　　　*　　　*

Several years passed.

Lukas grew bigger and became older.

One day his mum asked him if he'd like another cat.

'I've already got a cat,' Lukas told her. 'I have Night. Even if he's not around at the moment.'

'But he's been missing for several years now,' said Beatrice.

'That doesn't matter,' said Lukas. 'I don't want to have two cats. I have Night, even if he's not here.'

Lukas sometimes dreamed about Night. It was always the same dream, repeated over and over again. Night sat alone on top of his rock, it was nighttime, and the moon was shining down on him. He was sitting washing himself, stroking his paw over his face and licking hard at his fur. But suddenly he would prick up his ears, as if he'd heard something. In his dream, Lukas knew that he was what Night had heard. Then Lukas would be standing at the bottom of the rock, and he and Night would talk to each other, until everything faded away and vanished.

* * *

Night never came back, and it was a mystery where he'd got to. But even when Lukas had grown up, he would always stop every time he saw a cat, and entice it to come and be stroked. He knew that it wasn't Night. But it was as if every cat he came across had a little bit of Night in it. It was as if all the cats knew that Night was doing fine, that they had met him, and that he was sending greetings to Lukas through them.

'Say hello to Night,' Lukas used to say as he bent down to stroke the unknown cat. 'Tell him everything's fine here as well.'

Everybody who knew Lukas knew that he loved cats. No matter how ugly or vicious a cat might be, Lucas always bent down to stroke it. There were some people who thought Lukas could talk to cats.

He couldn't really, of course.

It was just that he could never forget Night.

As long as he lived, Lukas kept on thinking about Night, and kept seeing him wandering along the road, on the way to the mysterious yet wonderful Rainy-Weather Land.